SHE SMILED AT HIM AS SHE BEGAN TO UNBUTTON HER BLOUSE . . .

"You're telling me you've come to be a sort of stand-in?" Fargo asked.

"More like a lay-in," Karla answered, her voice laughing and warm.

"Good enough," Fargo nodded. "I like accuracy."

Her fingers undid another button as she said, "After all, you were lured here under false pretenses, you might say."

"No doubt about it," he agreed happily.

"Stacy Smith isn't going to make it up to you," Karla added.

"You're right," he said, and, as he watched her undo the few remaining buttons, Fargo smiled broadly, knowing Karla was a woman who could really reward a man for a job well done . . .

$1.2

Exciting Westerns by Jon Sharpe

The Trailsman

Beginnings . . . they bend the tree and they mark the man. Skye Fargo was born when he was eighteen. Terror was his midwife, vengeance his first cry. Killing spawned Skye Fargo, ruthless, cold-blooded murder. Out of the acrid smoke of gunpowder still hanging in the air, he rose, cried out a promise never forgotten.

The Trailsman, they began to call him all across the West: searcher, scout, hunter, the man who could see where others only looked, his skills for hire but not his soul, the man who lived each day to the fullest, yet trailed each tomorrow. Skye Fargo, the Trailsman, the seeker who could take the wildness of a land and the wanting of a woman and make them his own.

Nevada, 1861, when
the gambling was whether
a man could stay alive.
The southern foothills
of the Ruby Mountains . . .

1

"Dammit, Dixie, you promised me peace, quiet, and a good ride in the hay, nothing else," Fargo protested.

"You been getting that. Hell, we hardly been out of that bed for two days," the woman answered.

Fargo watched her as she stood naked beside the cabin window, peering out, concern digging a frown into her forehead. Dixie Treadwell had always been an ample woman, he recalled; even as a young girl ten years ago she was slightly heavy. Broad features surrounded by brown hair, a face more arresting than pretty. Large, overflowing breasts with big, pink-brown nipples, a rounded belly, rear a little heavy, and full-fleshed thighs, but all of a piece, all fitting together with an earthy sex, an easy-riding woman.

"Fargo, you can't just lay there and let this go on. Come look for yourself," Dixie called, her gaze staying focused out the window.

Fargo heaved a deep sigh from the bottom of his chest and swung long legs and a hard-muscled frame from the bed. Dixie had risen when she'd heard the distant shouts, and had stayed glued to the window.

"Hell, that's just a little boy out there," she said as Fargo started toward her. "He can't be more than twelve and those three big galoots are trying to run him down."

Fargo halted at her side, leaned against the smooth fullness of her body, and followed her gaze to the slope of a foothill just above the ridge that hid the little cabin from prying eyes. She was right about the boy, he saw; the youngster was most likely not past twelve. The boy rode a dark-brown quarterhorse and tried desperately to elude the three men who were trying to hem him in. He was doing a pretty good job of it, Fargo noted, as he wheeled his quarterhorse in tight, darting patterns. But he was tiring, Fargo saw, the three men coming closer with each attempt at rushing him.

"You get out there and see what that's all about, Fargo," Dixie demanded. "I don't like the look of it."

As he watched, Fargo saw the boy make a wrong turn and one of his pursuers move in fast. Panicked, the boy made another mistake, tried to send his horse in a straight spurt between the other two men. But the horse didn't have enough speed left in him and the two men had the angle in their favor. Fargo saw them converging on the boy and he turned from the window. "All right, you win," he muttered to Dixie. "I'll get dressed and have a look."

"They've got him," he heard Dixie cry out. "They've knocked him off his horse. Christ, they're kicking him." Fargo started to reach for his pants, halted at Dixie's scream. "There's no time to dress. Just get out there before they kill that kid."

"Shit," Fargo muttered as he grabbed his gun belt and strapped it on as he ran from the cabin. Clad only in the belt with the big Colt .45 in the holster, he vaulted onto the unsaddled Ovaro outside and sent the horse into a gallop. He felt the smooth warmth of the horse through his thighs and buttocks, the oneness of horse and rider the red man knew so well. The path to the slope led down and around the base of the foothill, far too long a way, he decided, and sent the pinto up a steep incline few horses could negotiate, and toward a ridge that would bring him directly onto the condalia-covered slope.

Damn Dixie, he swore silently. She had always been one for going to the aid of any stray, four-footed or two-footed. Until he rode into Jimson two days ago, he hadn't seen Dixie in five years. But the time vanished quickly, so quickly that she had pulled back. "I've a good reputation here in Jimson," she'd said. "The head of the women's church bazaar committee can't go shacking up with some stranger that rides into town."

"Not even an old friend?" he had said.

"Not even. Nobody here knows about the old days of Dixie Treadwell, and I intend to keep it that way," she'd answered.

"You want me to keep riding?" he had asked.

"You know I don't," Dixie had snapped. "I've done too much remembering over the years to let you just ride on." She'd told him about the cabin then, her own little hideaway, and he'd gone to it, was waiting there when she arrived.

The boy's sharp cry of pain broke into his thoughts as he topped the ridge. The three men had dismounted, one holding the boy on the ground and slapping his head back and forth while the other two watched. All three turned as Fargo rode across the slope. He saw the astonishment in their eyes and couldn't begrudge them that much.

"Jesus, I thought I'd seen everything," one said from under a dirty-gray stetson. The man holding the boy stared at the all-but-naked rider out of little button eyes and kept his knee on the boy's chest.

11

"Let the boy up," Fargo said, reining to a halt.

"Who the hell are you, some kind of freak?" the one with the dirty-gray hat asked. The third man just watched, his lined face grim.

Fargo's lips were a thin line and he silently swore at Dixie. It was more than a little hard to be impressive in his naked attire.

"Let the boy up," he repeated.

The man grinned from under the stetson. "I know, you wanted to prove you've got balls? Okay, we've seen 'em. Now get the hell out of here, freak," he said. He was too busy grinning to see the blue-ice in the naked man's eyes.

"I don't need clothes on to shoot," Fargo said softly.

The man's grin vanished, became a half-snarl. "Fuck off or I'll put a bullet up your bare ass," he said.

"Kill him," the one holding the boy growled.

Fargo saw the man with the stetson immediately go for his gun. He never got it out of its holster as the big black-haired man's Colt seemed to leap from its holster with a will of its own. The gun barked once and the man's head seemed to all but fly from his shoulders as he half-somersaulted backward, and suddenly the dirty-gray stetson became a dull red. The second man managed to get his gun out of the holster, but the big Colt moved a fraction of an inch to the left and barked again. The man went backward with a kind of strange shuffle before sinking to the ground to lay in a twisted heap.

Fargo saw the third man dive forward into a row of thick condalia shrub, taking the boy with him. There was no chance for a clean shot and Fargo executed a backward half-flip from the pinto, anticipating the two shots that came a split second later. Fargo rolled into a thicket of the

12

condalia, came up on his stomach, the Colt ready to fire. He saw the brush move a half-dozen yards away, but the man stayed out of sight with the boy. Fargo moved, winced. The rough thicket had jabbed him in the groin. Less than a half-minute passed before he heard the man's voice.

"You out there, throw your gun out," the man called.

Fargo stayed silent.

"The gun, throw it out or the kid gets it. I'll blast his damn head off," the man called again.

"No, you won't," Fargo called back.

"The hell I won't," he heard the man shout.

"He's your ace card only while he's alive. You shoot him and you're a dead man, guaranteed," Fargo returned. "You keep him alive and you stay alive." Fargo listened to the silence and knew the man cursed in angry frustration, all too aware the strange naked man had called his bluff correctly. "Let the boy go and you can ride away alive," he called.

"Just like that, eh?" the man returned.

"You've my word on it," Fargo said.

"Maybe that don't mean shit," the man replied.

Fargo nodded to himself. He could understand the man's answer. He'd probably give the same, if positions were reversed.

He thought for a moment, lifted his voice again. "You can take the boy in the saddle with you, ride a hundred yards. That's plenty far out of six-gun range. Let the boy go there and keep riding," Fargo said. He waited, let the man turn over the offer.

"What if I keep riding with him?" the man asked.

"You won't make another hundred yards, I promise you," Fargo said.

Another moment of silence and then the man's voice

called again, a new respect in it. "Who the hell are you, mister?" he asked.

"Fargo . . . Skye Fargo. Some call me the Trailsman," the big black-haired man answered.

"All right, I'm comin' out. Anything tricky and I'll blast the kid," the man called. Fargo stayed behind the shrub as he saw the man rise, a gun held to the boy's bloodied cheek. The man moved from the condalia with the boy held in front of him, backed toward his horse. He was perspiring, Fargo saw, his forehead shining, his little eyes blinking nervously.

Fargo remained out of sight as the man mounted his horse from the other side, kept the gun against the boy's face. He pulled the boy up with him, kept one thick arm around the boy's waist, using the slender figure as a shield. He sent the horse into a fast canter, and Fargo rose from the shrub and stepped to the Ovaro. He pulled himself onto the horse, his lake-blue eyes narrowed, held unwaveringly on the rider moving away. Fargo counted off yards, started to push his knees into the pinto's ribs when he saw the man halt and the small figure slip to the ground. Fargo sent the pinto forward as the man raced his horse away at a full gallop.

The boy was still standing when Fargo reached him, his young face bloodied and bruised. Fargo swung from the pinto. "You're safe now, son," he said as he put his hand on the boy's shoulder and felt the small figure tremble.

"Thanks to you, mister," the boy said, and Fargo saw his eyes flick over his nakedness.

"I usually wear more than this," Fargo said. He lifted the boy onto the pinto, swung on behind him, and turned the horse around. "Can you ride on your own?" he asked when he reached the boy's quarterhorse.

14

The boy nodded, climbed onto his horse as Fargo drew the pinto up alongside it. Fargo saw the boy eye him again from under swollen brows. The boy had been knocked around plenty, but he was still sharp, hurt but unshaken. There was a toughness in that slender frame, Fargo decided.

"You said your name was Fargo?" the boy questioned, and Fargo nodded. "Never saw anyone shoot that fast, Mr. Fargo," the boy said. "With or without clothes," he added.

"Follow me," Fargo said, turned the pinto down the long way. It was easier riding, and when he reached the little cabin, he saw Dixie, in skirt and blouse, rush out to meet them. Her round face was wreathed in horror as she saw the boy's bloodied and battered face.

"You just come with me," she said, helping him from the horse. "You must hurt all over."

"I'm all right," the boy said as Fargo saw him wince with pain. No fake bravery, he decided. Tough little customer, he concluded again as Dixie led the boy into the cabin.

Fargo took the quarterhorse to the side of the cabin and tethered the animal, let the Ovaro graze on his own. When he returned to the cabin, Dixie had washed the caked blood from the boy's face, had him lying on the bed with his shirt off. He seemed smaller, more the little boy with slender arms and a boy's unmuscled body. But the strength was there in the set of his little chin, a certain stoic quality in his dark-brown eyes set in a square face topped with short brown hair. Dixie was applying salve from a small crock to the boy's bruises.

"Powder made from the bark of the slippery elm mixed with lobelia," she said. "It'll take the pain out of those bruises in no time."

"Thank you, ma'am," the boy murmured.

"Call me Dixie," Fargo heard Dixie say. He pulled on shorts and trousers, then the rest of his clothes, and felt less foolish-looking. He leaned against the wall and the boy met his gaze.

"You want to tell us what this is all about?" Fargo said. "Start with your name."

"Bobby," the boy said. "Bobby Darrow."

"Who were those men, Bobby?" Fargo asked.

"I don't know," Bobby Darrow said. "They just started chasing me."

"For no reason?" Fargo questioned.

"Oh, they had a reason. They wanted the medicine," Bobby Darrow said.

"The medicine?" Fargo echoed.

"Yes, sir." Bobby nodded, his little face grave.

"You know what the men wanted, but you don't know who they were," Fargo said, and the boy nodded. "This isn't making a hell of a lot of sense, Bobby. Suppose we start over. What medicine?"

"The medicine for the wagon train," Bobby said.

Dixie had stopped rubbing the salve on him. "What wagon train, Bobby?" she cut in.

"The one up in the Ruby Mountains," the boy said.

"You came from a wagon train?" Dixie pressed.

"Yes, ma'am. I came to get the medicine and bring it back to them," Bobby answered.

"They sent you, a little boy?" Dixie frowned.

Bobby nodded gravely. "I was the only one who could go. Half the wagon train is real sick. There's some that have died. It was decided that the few men still well had to stay there. That's Shoshoni country up there. We've seen signs."

"Paiute and Nez Percé, too. Sometimes the Chiricahua Apache get up that far," Fargo said.

16

"What are they sick with, Bobby? Not the plague or smallpox?" Dixie asked anxiously.

"No, but there's a real bad fever, the killing kind, and chills and aching," Bobby said. "Doc Anderson, he's with the train, he was taking care of it pretty well until he ran out of medicine. Then folks started dying. The doc said it'd get worse unless he got some more medicine. He said there was a doctor in Jimson who used the kind of medicine he needed."

"In Jimson? That'd be Doc Bellows," Dixie said.

"Yes, ma'am, that's where I went," Bobby said.

"I still can't see sending a young boy." Dixie frowned again.

"There was nobody else, Miss Dixie. Besides, I was the lightest. I could make the best time on a good horse, and Doc said every minute counted. He gave me directions to Jimson and I went," Bobby said. "Only got lost twice," he added with a touch of pride.

"Tell me about those three men again," Fargo asked.

"Last night, after I left the doc's with the medicine, they came at me," Bobby said. "I got away from them in the dark and hid the medicine. I waited till morning and started out again. I thought they'd leave me alone when they saw I didn't have the medicine."

Fargo nodded. Bobby could think on his feet. He was shrewd as well as tough. "They say why they wanted the medicine?" he queried.

"No, sir. They just said they wanted it," Bobby answered.

"That medicine, did Doc Bellows tell you whether he had any more?" Dixie interjected.

"That was the last of it. He said it'd be a month before he got any more," Bobby said.

"There's your answer," Dixie said to Fargo. "They need

it for somebody or someplace, found out that Bobby had the last of it, and went after him for it."

"Maybe," Fargo muttered.

"Maybe?" Dixie questioned.

"Kind of a strange coincidence, their needing the same medicine at the same time," Fargo commented.

Dixie was digesting his words when Bobby's voice cut in. "Thank you both very much," the boy said, "but I've got to be moving on."

"Moving on?" Dixie frowned in protest as Bobby pulled on his shirt. "You're in no condition to go on."

"I don't feel too good, but I've got to go," Bobby said to her, his eyes wide. "I've lost enough time. I've got to get that medicine back to the wagons before it's too late."

"You think you can find your way back?" Dixie asked.

Fargo saw Bobby shrug, look suddenly uncertain. "I don't know. I have to try," he said, and Fargo saw Dixie's concern spiraling.

"And what about those men? One got away. He could be watching for you, maybe with others," Dixie said.

Bobby shrugged and tossed Dixie a glance of helpless bravery. "I'll have to chance it, Miss Dixie," he said.

Fargo's eyes narrowed. The kid was playing Dixie's built-in concern for all it was worth. Why? Fargo started to wonder when Bobby's next words supplied one reason.

"I wish I didn't have to go alone, but I can't do anything about that," he heard Bobby say, once more with touching bravery.

The little con man, Fargo muttered silently, and watched Dixie take the bait the way a trout takes a minnow.

"I can do something about it, Bobby," she said.

"Could you really, Miss Dixie?" Bobby said with just the right touch of grateful hope.

The little bastard, Fargo growled to himself. He was playing it to the hilt. Fargo saw Dixie turn to him and he knew exactly what she was going to say.

And exactly what he was going to answer.

2

Dixie kept her eyes fastened on the big man's chiseled face. "Fargo will go with you, Bobby," she said.

"Hell he will," Fargo growled. "He's got other plans."

"Such as?" Dixie frowned.

"Staying right here. You want me to spell the rest of it out in front of Bobby?" Fargo said.

He heard Bobby's voice cut in. "That's all right, Mr. Fargo. I understand," Bobby said. He managed to sound noble, Fargo swore. Dixie's quick glance at the boy was pure sympathy.

"You stay right there, Bobby," she said. "Excuse us for a minute." Sympathy gave way to spears in the glance she tossed Fargo. "Come outside," she snapped, and strode from the cabin. Fargo followed her to where, hands on hips, exasperation and anger in her every feature, she hissed words at him. "Dammit, Fargo, you can't mean what you just said," she flung out.

"Try me," he answered.

"You could go back and make love knowing what you just saw and heard?" Dixie asked, her eyes wide with angry astonishment.

"I'm not the world's keeper, honey," Fargo growled.

"How can you have such a big prick and such a small conscience?" she half-shouted.

"It works out fine. One doesn't get in the way of the other," he answered.

"This is an errand of mercy, Fargo," Dixie said.

"Go find a circuit-riding preacher," he returned.

"Can you really turn your back on a wagonload of sick people and a little boy?" Dixie pressed.

"Let's get something straight, honey. Lots of decent folks get themselves into trouble. That's life, that's the way it turns out sometimes. If I went chasing to help everybody that needed help, I'd be busy every day of the damn year. I'd starve to death, too. I've a little time between jobs and I figured spending it with you would be a damn nice way to do it. I don't see a damn thing wrong in that. As I said, honey, I'm not the world's keeper."

"It's not wrong the way you put it, but it's not right, not when people need help and you can help them," Dixie said, stubbornness setting into her broad face.

"Damn, you should've been a Methodist preacher, Dixie," Fargo rasped. "As for that little boy, he's tough, shrewd, and tricky. He made his way to Jimson and he'll make his way back. He's played you to do just what you're doing. He wants me to go with him. I don't know why, but that's what he wants."

"Of course he wants you to go with him. That bush-whacker is probably still watching for him. He's scared," Dixie answered.

"He may be a lot of things, but scared isn't one of them," Fargo said. "It's something more than just the men and the medicine."

"You're always looking for hidden motives. You're the most suspicious man I ever knew, Fargo," Dixie snapped.

"Comes from being right most times," he returned.

"Most times." Dixie sniffed. "Well, I'll tell you one thing, Skye Fargo, I'm not going to be the reason you won't help those poor people."

"Meaning what?"

"You stay here and you'll be staying alone," she threw back.

"Playing pussy power?" Fargo speared.

"Call it whatever you like, but I'm not staying," Dixie said between tight lips.

"You can't be the world's keeper, either, Dixie," Fargo said, not ungently.

"I don't care about the world. I care about that little boy and a wagon train of sick people depending on him," Dixie said. "And if he has other reasons for wanting you to go with him, I don't give a damn about them either."

"Dammit, Dixie, you always were one stubborn female when you got yourself all worked up about something," Fargo said.

"I'd rather be stubborn than selfish," she returned haughtily.

Fargo let a long sigh escape him as he shook his head slowly. "Seeing as how you've given me no reason to stay, I might as well see to the boy," he said.

Dixie's arms were around him instantly, her big breasts warm softness pressing against his chest. "Make it up to you when you get back. I promise," she murmured into his cheek.

"You better," Fargo growled. "Get that damn kid out here."

Dixie disappeared into the cabin and Bobby came out on the run moments later as Fargo saddled the pinto.

"Thanks, Mr. Fargo," Bobby said. "I understand about your not wanting to leave."

"You do?" Fargo said as he tightened the cinch under the Ovaro's belly.

"Yes, I've been around," Bobby said.

Fargo tossed a glance at the boy. "I expect you have," Fargo growled.

"You won't be sorry you came with me," Bobby said.

"Why's that?" Fargo questioned.

Bobby moved closer, lowered his voice confidentially. "I didn't want to say it in front of Miss Dixie, but you can have Miss Smith when we get back to the wagon train," he said in a half-whisper. He stayed unruffled under Fargo's glance.

"I can? Who the hell is Miss Smith?" Fargo asked.

"She's sort of my guardian," Bobby said.

Fargo frowned. "Your guardian? What makes you think I can have her?"

"She told me I could promise that if I found somebody who could really help us," Bobby answered.

Fargo let the skepticism show in his eyes, but Bobby seemed unbothered by it. "We'll talk more later. Let's get that medicine now," Fargo said.

"Right, Mr. Fargo," Bobby answered as he climbed onto the quarterhorse.

"Forget the 'mister,' " Fargo growled. "Makes me feel old." He let Bobby lead and saw the boy head back toward Jimson, followed in silence. They neared the outskirts of town when the boy veered his horse toward a shack a half-dozen yards from the road, a place with the roof caved in, the door hanging by one hinge, a shack as much falling down as it was standing. Bobby jumped to the ground and ran inside the shack as Fargo waited on the pinto. Only a half-minute had passed when he heard Bobby's scream from inside the shack.

"It's not here. It's gone," Bobby shouted, and Fargo slid

from the pinto and hurried inside the shack. The place smelled of rotted wood and decay, of mushroom spores and damp earth that never had sunlight to dry out. Bobby stood in a corner, his face filled with shock. "I hid it right here, under those old boxes," he said.

Fargo pushed the boxes with the toe of his boot as Bobby stared at the spot. "Nothing here," Fargo said.

"It's gone. He came back here and found it," Bobby said.

"Why would he know to come back here looking?" Fargo questioned.

"This is where I gave them the slip last night," Bobby said. "The third man, he must have put two and two together and figured I had to have hid it around here."

Fargo nodded agreement. He turned and stepped outside, dropped down to one knee as his eyes scanned the ground.

Bobby followed him out. "It had to be that. It had to be him," the boy said.

"He had company," Fargo muttered, pointed to the prints in the ground. "Two horses," he said, rising to his feet. "These prints are fresh. They don't have that much a start. We can catch them."

"Oh, boy, could we?" Bobby's eyes sparkled.

"We better, if you want that medicine back," Fargo said. "Let's move."

Bobby flew onto the quarterhorse as Fargo began to follow the tracks. The two sets of hoofprints stayed at two, he saw. The two men weren't pushing their horses. Obviously they felt secure. Fargo nodded in satisfaction. It was always easier to track someone who felt safe.

The afternoon slid quickly toward an end and Bobby's voice echoed the frown that had begun to dig into Fargo's brow. "They're going up into the mountains," the boy said. "This is the way I'd be heading back to the wagon train."

"Lots of trails start out the same way but end differently," Fargo said. "Let's talk some. What are you and your sort-of-guardian doing in that wagon train?"

"She's taking me to an aunt and uncle in Thunder Rock at the foot of the Amagosa Range," Bobby said.

"The Amagosa Range? That'd be just across the California border," Fargo said.

"Yes, sir," Bobby answered.

"That's where the train is headed?" Fargo questioned, and the boy nodded. Fargo's lips pursed in thought. They'd not have an easy road—south once they got out of the Ruby Mountains, staying just east of the Shoshoni Mountains with plenty of hot country waiting to fatigue horses. Plenty of rattlers, too, the kind that crawled and the kind that walked.

Fargo pulled to a halt as they came to a half-circle with a small pool of water that bubbled up from an underground spring. "They're not far ahead of us now," he said. "It'll be night soon. They'll be stopping."

"Maybe they'll ride through the night," Bobby said.

"No, they'll be making camp," Fargo said.

"How do you know?" Bobby persisted.

"They're looking for a spot. They were going to make camp here," Fargo said, his eyes reading the marks on the ground. "One of them dismounted."

"Why didn't they? It seems a fine spot," Bobby said.

"Why don't you check out that little spring," Fargo said blandly, and watched Bobby slide from his horse, lay down on his stomach at the edge of the spring. Suddenly he pulled back, coughed, shook his head to look up with his eyes tearing.

"Yeeeuuck!" he gasped, pushed himself to his feet. "That smells awful."

"Figured it might. It's a sulfur spring," Fargo said, and moved the pinto forward. Bobby caught up to him as he watched the double set of tracks continue to lead up into the mountain. "How far do you figure we are from your train?" Fargo asked the boy.

"By day, maybe another four hours," Bobby answered. "There's a turn by a broken Sierra juniper. I'm lost if we miss it."

"We won't," Fargo said.

"Why are they heading up the same way I'd go back?" Bobby asked.

"Maybe they are going to your wagon train," Fargo thought aloud.

"Why?" Bobby questioned.

"Maybe they figure to sell the medicine to the others there," Fargo said, and saw Bobby's frown of shock. "Sure, it's rotten, but I've seen rottener things men do to each other," he said. "If so, they had to know there was sickness in the train and that means they were watching. Why?"

Bobby shrugged his small shoulders. "Don't know why. It's just a wagon train," he said.

Maybe and maybe not, Fargo reckoned. Bobby was bright, shrewd, resourceful, but he was still a twelve-year-old, far from a mature observer. The men had been watching the wagons, had gone after the boy when he left to get the medicine. There had to be a reason. They couldn't know the fever was going to hit the train. He considered coincidence and shook it away. Too neat.

"Tell me more about the train, Bobby," he said as they rode upward through the last of the twilight. "How many wagons?"

"There were eight. Some folks shared wagons," Bobby said. "Then all three of the Scully brothers died from the fever. Old lady Epworth, too. She rode with the Scully brothers."

"Everybody going to cross over the California border?" Fargo questioned.

"Yes, sir," Bobby said.

Fargo pulled the pinto into a little glen of aspen and swung to the ground. "We'll sleep some here," he said. Bobby dismounted and took his bedroll down. "You have anything to eat with you?" Fargo asked.

"Some beef jerky," Bobby said. "Enough for now."

Fargo spread his own bedroll, ate some dried buffalo meat he had with him, and stretched out. "Tell me some more about Miss Smith," he said casually as Bobby prepared to turn in. "You like her?"

"I hate her." The answer was snapped back, an instant reaction, and Fargo saw the boy's face had set tightly.

"Why?" he asked, keeping his tone mild.

"I've my reasons," Bobby said, his lips hardly moving.

"She too strict?" Fargo questioned.

"That's part of it," Bobby spat out.

Fargo nodded, decided not to press that further. "She have a first name?" he asked.

"Stacy," Bobby said with distaste. "Fancy name and fancy airs."

"She the only single woman in the train?" Fargo queried.

"No," Bobby answered.

"She running the train?" Fargo asked.

"Nobody's running it," Bobby snapped.

"Then how come she told you to make that offer?" he slid at the boy, his eyes sharp, and he saw Bobby hesitate, grope for an answer.

"That's just the way she is," Bobby said, more than a little lamely.

Fargo smiled as he turned on his side. "Get some sleep," he muttered. He watched Bobby wrap himself in his bedroll, heard the even sounds of his breathing in minutes. The boy was still playing his own little game, Fargo mused as he turned on his side and slept, the big Colt at his fingertips.

He woke to his inner alarm clock as the night was just beginning to welcome the day. He rose, washed quickly with his canteen, and bent over to shake Bobby's sleeping form. The boy snapped awake at once. "We ride," he said, and Bobby sat up, pushed himself free of his bedroll.

Fargo waited in the saddle as the boy rolled his gear up and pulled himself onto the quarterhorse. Fargo sent the Ovaro upward along a narrow path and watched the dawn come to assert its right to rule the day. Fargo had picked up the trail already, followed it over a ledge of stone, and reined up sharply to look across a flat stretch of shale and scrub brush. Bobby halted alongside him, followed his gaze to where two men were starting to rise from their blankets.

Fargo dismounted, started forward in a crouch, the Colt in his hand, darted behind an outcrop of shale amid the trees. He felt Bobby's small form against him as he halted and dropped to one knee. The men were starting to gather their gear and the boy's eyes espied the canvas sack on the ground.

"That's it, that's the medicine," Bobby whispered, excitement shaking his voice.

Fargo moved again, slid his big form through a narrow crevice in the shale to come out only a few yards from the two men. Once again, he felt Bobby against him. The nearest man's little button eyes blinked as he scanned the camp area.

"Get the bag, Len," he said.

Fargo raised the Colt as the other man, a thin-faced, wiry figure, started to bend down to pick up the canvas sack.

"Leave it be," Fargo said, his voice soft yet made of steel.

The man froze in place with his hand outstretched, an inch from the bag, his body bent half over. The other one proved to be the surprise as he whirled, gun out, firing wildly yet spraying hot lead in a deadly volley.

Fargo dropped to the ground, pulling Bobby with him, his reaction instant and automatic. The big Colt fired, two shots that slammed into the figure. Fargo saw the little button eyes blink as the man doubled forward almost in two. The man's hands clasped his abdomen and grew red. He toppled forward to hit the ground with his forehead, fall on his side still doubled in two.

It all took but seconds, yet it was enough for the thin-faced figure to seize the canvas sack and dive into the brush. Fargo heard him roll, come up on his feet, anticipated the shot that followed, and stayed down in the edge of the brush line. Motioning for Bobby to stay, Fargo waited, his ears straining for any sound. Slowly, he moved, pulled himself along the ground, halted, listened, and heard the other man move in the brush. The man pushed a half-dozen feet deeper into the brush and fell silent. Fargo peered across the clearing to the brush on the other side, his eyes moving slowly along the tops of the dark-green leaves. He caught the faint movement halfway around the edge of the clearing, the brush shimmering from side to side. His eyes flicked to where Bobby lay on the ground nearby, out of the line of any return fire, and he raised the

Colt, aimed just under the tops of the brush that still quivered. He let his finger tighten against the trigger and the Colt exploded, a single shot that tore through the brush.

"*Goddamn!*" he heard the man curse and heard the sound of his body crashing backward. But there was no pain in the curse, only surprise and fear. The shot had missed but come close enough.

"That's to let you know," Fargo called.

There was a moment of silence. "Let me know what?" the man called back.

"That I don't have to see you to kill you," Fargo said.

The man fell silent again for a long pause. "You're Fargo, the one they call the Trailsman," the voice said.

"That's right," Fargo answered.

"Charley told me about how fast you were," the man said.

"He won't be telling anybody else," Fargo commented with flat grimness.

"Look, I'll deal, mister," the man called.

"You need cards to deal," Fargo returned.

"I've got cards," the man replied. "You want the medicine. You let me ride out of here and you can have it."

"I'll have it when I'm finished putting six slugs in you," Fargo said.

"You get off another shot and I'll spill out every damn bottle," the man returned. "You won't just be killing me. You'll be finishing off every man, woman, and child on that wagon train. There'll be no medicine for anybody."

Fargo felt the curse spiral up inside himself. The bastard had cards, all right, he grunted.

The man's voice rose again. "I got nothin' to lose, Fargo. I go, so does the medicine and the wagon train," he said.

Fargo swore again in silent anger, the man's words all too true. He had nothing to lose, and that was his ace card. Fargo's answer came through lips that were but a thin slit across his face. "I'm listening," he said. "Deal."

"I get my horse and I leave the bag on the ground," the man said. "I keep going. You've got the medicine."

Fargo rifled through his own options, came up with nothing safe. He forced words through his lips. "Get your horse," he said. "No tricks."

"No tricks. I'm no fool," the man returned, and Fargo watched the brush quiver as the man began to work his way back to his horse, staying in the cover of the brush. Fargo stayed low also as he pushed his own way back to where Bobby crouched beside a tree.

"You stay right there," Fargo told the boy as he positioned himself against the grainy gray bark of a burr oak. He saw the thin-faced figure rise from the brush on the other side of the small clear space. The man moved to his horse, stayed on the far side of the mount, and Fargo watched his eyes peer over the saddle. The man stayed close to the horse, using the animal almost as a shield, and seemed to adjust the stirrup leather. Fargo raised the Colt, took aim, his finger resting against the trigger. He waited, watched as the man took another moment with the stirrup and finally pulled himself up into the saddle. The man held the canvas sack in one hand and Fargo saw him move the horse a few paces. Fargo's finger on the trigger tightened a fraction and the big Colt was trained dead-center on the long figure. The man halted the horse, leaned far out of the saddle, and his hand but a foot from the ground, he dropped the sack onto the grass. He straightened and sent the horse forward in a gallop, not looking back, hunching down in the saddle as he raced away through the trees.

Fargo straightened, holstered the Colt, and walked to the sack as Bobby ran out to join him. He lifted the canvas sack and handed it to the boy. "Hang on to it," he said.

Bobby took the sack, held it up for a moment, and Fargo saw his small face take on a frown. "It seems heavier than it was," Bobby said, hefting the sack in his hand. He glanced up to see Fargo's mouth turn hard. Dropping to one knee, Bobby pulled the top of the sack open, unwinding the rope that held it closed. He peered inside, turned the sack upside down, and Fargo watched the rocks spill out onto the ground.

"Son of a bitch," Fargo muttered. "You stay here," he ordered Bobby. "If I don't come back, look to your own neck." He brought his hand down on the pinto's rump, a sharp, stinging blow, and the horse leaped forward, hit a full gallop in seconds. Fargo, his lake-blue eyes cold as ice floes, sent the pinto racing through the woods. With quick, flicking glances, he picked up the man's trail of broken branch ends, trampled brush, a bed of red russulas crushed by hooves.

The man rode in wild flight with no time to cover tracks, and Fargo spurred the pinto forward with reckless abandon through the woods that grew thicker. He'd gone perhaps a thousand yards when he glimpsed his quarry and saw the man turn in the saddle, raise his six-gun.

Fargo dropped low over the saddle horn as he kept the pinto plunging forward. The man's first two bullets were high, the third shot lower but to the right. Fargo raised his head up just enough to see the man bring his horse to a halt to get a steadier shot. Fargo kept the pinto racing forward as he slid down the far side of the horse. He hit the ground on all fours as the pinto plunged almost directly at the other horse, saw the surprise in the man's eyes as his shots grazed the top of the empty saddle instead of slamming into his pursuer. Surprise became panic in the thin face and the man leaped out of the saddle to avoid becoming a sitting target.

Fargo used the moment to push himself up, dart forward, dive behind a tree only a few yards from where the man landed. His quarry fired off another shot at once as Fargo pressed himself behind the tree trunk. He continued to keep the big Colt holstered, reached an arm out, and yanked it back.

The man fired at once and Fargo's tiny smile was thin. The sixth shot, he commented silently. Eight seconds to reload if he was real good. Ten to twelve seconds were more likely. Fargo raced from behind the tree, reached the other man just as he'd loaded the sixth bullet into the chamber of his gun, saw the fear in the man's eyes as he started to bring the gun up.

Fargo twisted himself sideways in midair as he dived forward, felt the first shot graze his side, and then he was atop the man, one hand clamping down on his gun arm, forcing it back. "I want you alive," he hissed as the man's second shot went harmlessly into the air. Half atop the long, lean figure, he brought his other arm around, jammed it against the man's throat.

"Goddamn . . . aaagh . . ." the man gasped, used his free hand to try to tear at the forearm that was closing off his breath. The thin lean figure had its own brand of wiry strength and Fargo felt the man's hand pull his forearm back enough to relieve the pressure against his throat. "Bastard," he heard the man gasp out through the welcome rush of air in his throat.

Fargo pressed the man's gun arm back against a rock, shifted his grip upward, and bent the man's wrist backward over the edge of the rock.

"Ow, Jesus," the man cried out in pain, and Fargo saw

the gun fall from his hand. He rolled, taking the lean figure with him, flung the man sideways as he leaped to his feet. He moved forward, brought a short, chopping blow downward. It caught the man along the side of the jaw, and he pitched forward onto both knees. Fargo stepped forward, reached a hand down to clamp it around the back of his neck when the thin, wiry figure bolted forward with the impact of a steel spring uncoiling.

Fargo felt his knees buckle as the man slammed into him. He went down and the man leaped up, rained blows with the speed of a flailing windmill. Fargo blocked most, but enough got through to drive him backward as he tried to regain his feet. The thin figure had a steel-wire strength driven by fear, and Fargo's head snapped back as three blows landed. He half-turned, felt the man leap on his back, wrap both arms around his neck. Fargo, his own fury exploding, pushed up with his powerful leg muscles, used both palms to execute a forward somersault. He landed on his back, the thin figure beneath him, and heard the man's gasp and the rush of his breath driven from him. Fargo tore from the man's grip, whirled, brought a driving right in an arc as the man started to half-rise. It caught the man's jaw and drove his head backward into the ground.

Fargo pulled himself to his feet as the thin figure lay before him, twitching, and he saw the man lift his head, shake the cobwebs from his brain. Fargo reached both hands down to yank him to his feet when he caught the glint of metal. He leaped backward as the man's right hand came up with a short-handled skinning knife.

The blade sliced upward and just missed raking Fargo's abdomen as he drew in his stomach. Off balance after the upward thrust, the thin figure tried to turn, but the Trailsman's blow, a tremendous downward chop, caught

34

him across the back of the neck. The man fell forward and Fargo heard his painracked gasp, instantly followed by a breathy groan as the thin figure lay facedown on the ground, one hand half under him.

"Goddamn," Fargo swore as he pushed the figure over with the toe of his boot. The man's hand still clutched the handle of the skinning knife, but the blade was buried to its hilt in his chest. Fargo watched the man's lips move, try to form words, but only little hissing sounds came from him. His eyes closed and Fargo watched his hand fall away from the handle of the knife. The thin figure gave a last shudder and lay still.

"Goddamn," Fargo swore again. He leaned forward and pulled the man's shirt open to see the leather sheath for the skinning knife on the inside of his belt.

Fargo rose, let out a sigh as he turned to the man's horse. He opened the saddlebag. The bottles of medicine were tucked inside, put there when it seemed the stirrup leather was being adjusted. Fargo turned from the bag, bent down, and went through the man's pockets. He found only loose change, a tobacco pouch, and a receipt for a pair of Levi's. He rose, called the pinto, and the gleaming black-and-white horse trotted into sight. Fargo swung up into the saddle, took the reins of the other horse in hand, and rode back to where the small figure still waited anxiously beside a tree.

Bobby broke into a run when he saw the Ovaro, met Fargo at the edge of the clearing with the canvas sack in his hand.

"The medicine's in the saddlebag. Put it in your sack," Fargo said.

"You find out anything from him?" Bobby asked as he began to transfer the bottles of medicine.

"Nothing," Fargo said, and decided to keep his thoughts

to himself. Little Bobby was still holding back things and he wanted that cleared up first. But he was bothered. Something didn't set right. They'd gone to a hell of a lot of effort to get their hands on that medicine. Selling it back wouldn't bring that much, not from the average wagon train. Unless this one was different, made up of rich men instead of the usual poor ones. He'd find that out soon, Fargo pondered as Bobby finished putting the bottles into the canvas sack.

"Tie the sack onto your saddle horn," Fargo said, and the boy obeyed. He'd just finished when Fargo's body grew tight and he put a finger to his lips. Bobby, his eyes wide on the big man, froze against his horse. Fargo strained his ears for another moment and slid from the pinto. Taking the horse by the reins, he motioned for Bobby to follow as he led the way deeper into the woods, halting at a dense thicket of red cedar. He helped Bobby push the quarterhorse behind the thick leaves.

"I didn't hear anything," Bobby whispered.

"You have to educate your ears the way you educate your mind," Fargo said. He settled down on one knee, his eyes peering through the denseness of the scaly leaves. He saw the horsemen appear, file into the small clearing, and he counted five riders. Two dismounted and began to search the clearing, their voices carrying to where he watched.

"Here's Len," one said. "Dead, just like Charley."

"Nothin' else here, damn," the second man said.

"Keep looking," one of the men on horseback ordered, and the two men on foot scuffed their way around the clearing.

"Nothin'," one said. "It's not here. Let's get back and tell Maxey. He'll be mad as hell, but it's not our fault. Somehow, the goddamn kid's got away with it."

Fargo watched as the men mounted their horses and the five riders filed back the way they had come. He rose when they were out of earshot and swung onto the pinto. "Let's go, Bobby," he said as he moved the horse from the dense thicket. He set out at right angles, away from the path the five horsemen had taken. Their appearance had reinforced the gnawing apprehension inside him. The medicine was drawing too much attention just to be sold back for a few dollars. There were strange undercurrents, he felt more than understood, his instinct sending him warning signals . . . and he'd learned long ago not to turn his back on instinct.

He headed upward through the mountains, stayed away from clear slopes and open plateaus, and executed a wide circle to bring them back on the path they had been following. He let Bobby take the lead then, and when Bobby came to the broken juniper, he laughed in satisfaction and his eyes were bright as he tossed a glance at the big man beside him. "How's that for keeping a trail?" he said.

"Good enough." Fargo smiled and followed as Bobby hurried his horse past the tree and on up a narrow, steep passage. Fargo stayed back to give the quarterhorse slipping room as he negotiated the sharp incline. The land offered little but hard riding for the rest of the day, and Fargo called a halt at a mountain stream as the afternoon began to wear down. He let the horses drink and cool their ankles, stretched out beside the stream, and watched Bobby as the boy stared into the burbling waters. A tightness had come into Bobby's face, his smooth features becoming somehow drawn. "Much farther?" Fargo asked.

"No," Bobby said, not looking up from the stream.

Fargo's eyes narrowed as he studied the boy, the tension very definitely in the small, smooth face. He decided to leave his questions for Bobby still unasked. The boy was growing nervous as they neared their destination. He seemed to expect something more than a hero's welcome. "Something bothering you, Bobby?" Fargo asked with casual mildness.

"No," Bobby snapped out, tossed a quick glance, but the big man's face showed only relaxed curiosity. "Nothin' bothering me."

"Good," Fargo commented, and watched the boy's face give the lie to his words. "Let's get moving, then," he said as he rose and led the Ovaro from the stream. They rode on, higher into the mountains, and the day was beginning to edge dusk when the wagons came into view, camped in a line against an uneven wall of red shale. Fargo followed as Bobby rode toward the nearest end of the line of wagons and he saw a man step from the last wagon, a thin, stooped figure with but a few wisps of gray hair coming down over his ears from a largely bald pate. The man wore a stethoscope around his neck and he looked up in surprise out of eyes that peered from over deep, hanging sockets of flesh, a face that held perpetual tiredness in it.

Bobby spurred the quarterhorse forward and waved the sack high in the air. "I got it, Doc," he shouted, and the man's tired face managed to take on a note of excitement. Bobby handed him the canvas sack and the doctor opened it, took one of the bottles out.

"Thank God, thank God," the man murmured, and Fargo saw him look up at Bobby, a frown touching his brow. "There's a lot that'll be said to you, Bobby, but for now I'll just say thank you," the doc stated.

"This is Fargo," Bobby introduced. "I wouldn't be here except for him."

"Then we're forever in your debt, sir," the doctor said, taking in the big man before him. "I'm Dr. Anderson.

We'll talk tomorrow. Right now I want to get everyone a shot of this medicine."

Fargo nodded and the doctor disappeared into his wagon, emerged in moments with his little black bag and the canvas sack. Fargo dismounted as the doctor entered the next wagon in line and he let his eyes move across the wagons with a critical sweep. Only one filled the requirements for a good, long-haul traveling wagon, a big Conestoga in the center of the line, shining new, outfitted with new canvas, its heavy wheels hardly nicked. The others, he frowned, were a sorry collection of makeshift vehicles.

He saw a platform-spring grocery wagon, sides still painted bright green, the hardwood roof a dark red and curtains hung over the two small windows at the front. It rested behind a big, unwieldy Owensboro mountain wagon with the oversize rear wheels, which had been outfitted with a canvas cover over squared-off wood frames. Two similarly fitted Studebaker farm wagons were next, a gray one and a tan one, followed by a big stake-sided dray with canvas wrapped around the stakes to form enclosed sides and roof. A light baggage wagon came next with wooden sides that had been built onto it to more or less enclose it with canvas flaps at the front and rear. The farthest wagon of the line was an adapted baker's wagon with its sliding doors and drop windows. He grimaced at the elliptic springs and wondered how they'd held up this far.

He was still grimacing in disgust when a girl stepped out of the gray Studebaker farm wagon, her eyes holding on him at once, flicking to Bobby and back to him.

"I brought the medicine, Miss Karla," Bobby said, and Fargo caught a note of defensiveness in the boy's tone.

"I heard what you said to Doc Anderson, Bobby," the young woman remarked, her eyes staying on the big man's handsome, chiseled face. She stayed on the top step of the wagon and Fargo took in black hair that hung loosely to her shoulders, brown eyes that held more experience than the unlined features of her face indicated. She had a nice mouth, full lips with a strong jaw beneath them, features a little broad but not without an earthy appeal. She moved down from the tailgate of the wagon and Fargo watched modest breasts swinging gracefully in unison under a white cotton blouse that tucked into ample hips.

"Karla Corrigan," she said.

"Skye Fargo," the big man answered.

"They call him the Trailsman," Fargo heard Bobby offer as he met Karla Corrigan's frankly approving glance that traveled up and down his hard-packed frame.

"You go around doing good deeds, Trailsman?" Karla Corrigan asked, and the worldly-wise amusement stayed in her eyes.

"Sometimes it just works out that way," Fargo said.

Her eyes went to Bobby, a suddenly hard glance. "You did it and that's enough for me. I don't think it'll be enough for Stacy Smith," she said to the boy.

Bobby's face tightened. "I don't care," he muttered.

Doc Anderson stepped from the second wagon, paused before entering the next in line. "You're next, Karla. Everybody's getting a shot, sick or not," he said.

He vanished into the wagon and Fargo's eyes saw the sliding door of the baker's wagon at the far end of the line come open. The night had lowered itself enough to leave little light, and he barely made out the figure that stepped from the wagon but he saw a flash of blond hair. The figure came toward him with a brisk stride, took form, became tall and slender, long breasts that touched sharp points in a thin silk blouse. The hair became dark blond, almost a light brown and worn in a pony tail. A thin, straight nose centered high cheekbones and finely etched lips echoed the classic beauty of a face marred only by an icy severity. The young woman halted, her eyes frost blue as they drilled into Bobby.

The boy glowered back, Fargo saw. "I got it," Bobby growled.

"That's supposed to make everything all right?" the young woman said.

"I brought it back. That ought to mean something," Bobby said doggedly.

"It means you were lucky," the young woman said, ice on her every word. "Not smart, not right, just lucky."

"Hold on, honey," Fargo heard himself cut in. "Seems to me he deserves a thank you at least, whatever the reasons."

Stacy Smith turned the frost-blue eyes on him, disdain in their round orbs. "This is not your affair. Kindly stay out of it, whoever you are," she snapped.

Fargo heard Karla Corrigan's voice answer. "He's Fargo. Seems he's the reason Bobby got back with the medicine," she said.

Stacy Smith's eyes didn't lose their disdain, only a faint edge of their frost. "I see. I'm sure everyone joins me in being grateful to you for that," she said. "But this is still a private matter." She returned her eyes to Bobby. "Go to the wagon. We'll talk more about this there."

"We've something to talk about," Fargo said to her.

She lifted her brows slightly as she glanced at him. "We do?" she questioned frostily. "I know of nothing that can't wait till morning."

Fargo shrugged and watched Stacy Smith as she strode away, a nice, narrow-hipped rear, he took note. He smiled to himself. She managed to make even her rear disdainful, holding the soft little mounds in tightly as she hurried away. He turned to Karla Corrigan, saw her eyes studying

41

him. "I still say the kid deserves a vote of thanks," Fargo said. "He did what you all sent him to do."

A little smile toyed with the corners of Karla Corrigan's wide mouth. "Nobody sent him to do anything," she said.

Fargo stared back, her words turning with mocking slowness in the air.

3

Fargo rested on his bedroll under the star-flecked sky. He had gone up higher into the mountains, found a spot that let him look down on the wagons below, only dim-gray canvas shapes in the night. He was more intrigued than angered as his conversation with Karla Corrigan hung in his mind. He'd found his voice after his initial surprise. "You want to run that past me again?" he had asked.

"I said nobody sent him," she had repeated.

"Fill in the spaces," he had snapped.

"There was a lot of arguing about who'd go," Karla had said. "Doc Anderson had written out directions to Jimson and we all knew someone had to go. But it was a bad scene, everybody wanting the medicine and most everybody afraid to risk their necks going for it. We'd argued half the night when suddenly Bobby grabbed the directions from Doc Anderson and lit out on his quarterhorse. He was gone before anyone could get themselves together."

Fargo's lips pursed as the conversation hung a moment longer and then he let it slip away as he focused thoughts on Bobby. The boy's story about being sent for the medicine hadn't even been a half-truth. It had been an outright lie, and it explained why Bobby had grown so tense as they neared the camp. But there was too much else it didn't explain. He'd be having his own talk with Bobby Darrow come the morrow, Fargo decided as he lay back, closed his eyes, and let sleep shut out the world.

He came awake twice during the night, once with the soft sound of a porcupine padding nearby and once with the low, throaty growl of a mountain lion. Too close, his hand had drawn the big Colt up until he heard the cat move on along a ledge. When the new sun came, he sat up, stretched, saw a trickle of a mountain stream that dropped waterfall-fashion from the rocks above. He used it to wash and let his clothes dry on a rock under the early sun. He relaxed till the morning was full, dressed, and rode leisurely down to the wagons.

The camp had come alive, small knots of people in front of two of the wagons, and he saw the small form detach itself from the others, run toward him as he reined to a halt and dismounted.

" 'Morning, Fargo," Bobby called, his face bright with excitement. "I've been telling everybody about you," the boy said.

Doc Anderson came forward and his tired face held a faint tinge of animation. "I guess, besides Bobby, I'm the official greeter, even though we met last night. We are indeed grateful for your help," the man said. "I'd like to introduce you to those well enough to say hello now."

Fargo nodded, saw Stacy Smith at the doctor's right, looking cool and fresh as a mountain spring, her dark-blond hair echoing the yellow shirt she wore over black Levi's. "This is Stacy Smith, Bobby's guardian," the doctor said.

"We met briefly last night," Stacy Smith said. She had learned how to smile and be distant at the same time,

Fargo took note. But he saw the faint tint of color touch her cheeks as she saw his eyes linger on the two tiny points pressed outward on the yellow shirt. Fargo turned away, let his gaze follow Doc Anderson as the physician motioned to a man standing beside two girls about twelve years old and a woman on the other side of the girls.

"Sam Johnson and Kate Johnson," the doctor said. "The youngsters are Abby and Ada." The Johnsons obviously belonged with the tan Studebaker farm wagon. Sam Johnson had a rugged, creased face and the hands of a smithy, his wife a sturdy woman with her hair worn curled up atop her head in a bun.

"The doc said the medicine got to us just in time. We're much obliged," Sam Johnson said.

"Glad I could help," Fargo said with a twinge of conscience. His eyes glanced over at the young woman who stepped from the gray Studebaker farm wagon, black hair glistening in the sun, her blouse unbuttoned down to the third button.

"You met Karla last night," the doc said, and Karla Corrigan slid a slow smile his way that managed to be quietly tantalizing.

A man emerged from the platform-spring grocery wagon, swinging to the ground to land on the balls of his feet, hands on his hips, a sardonic half-smile on a young face that was handsome despite the cruel twist of his mouth. He moved forward with a swagger.

"So you're the big gunfighter," he said, not hiding the sneer in his voice.

"No gunfighter," Fargo demurred.

"Bobby's been telling everybody how fast you are," the man said, the swagger in his voice as well as in his stance.

Fargo half-shrugged.

"I figure the kid's easy to impress," the man said.

"Probably," Fargo agreed pleasantly, and heard Doc Anderson interrupt.

"This is Darrell Rumford," the physician said.

Fargo ignored the challenge in the man's stare, lifted his glance as the girl stepped out of the grocery wagon. A thin body, breasts little high mounds that hardly protruded from under a gray dress, she had brown hair pulled back tight, pleasant-enough features that might have made her pretty were it not for the mousy, cowed air about her. He saw the reason for it as Darrell Rumford spun around to her.

"I told you not to come out till I called you," he spat at her. The girl seemed to shrink in, her eyes cast down at the ground. But she stayed unmoving, Fargo noted. Darrell Rumford turned back to him, his voice heavy with sarcasm. "I don't let just anybody meet my beautiful little wife," he said. "This here is Emmy. Say hello to the man, Emmy."

Fargo nodded and saw Emmy's eyes lift, her manner made of subservience, but for the briefest instant he thought he detected a flicker of sharpness in her light-brown orbs. But she lowered her eyes before he could be certain.

"You can talk to the man, Emmy. You got permission." Darrell Rumford laughed, a nasty sound. Emmy remained silent, her eyes downward.

Fargo saw more than embarrassment in the others as they looked on. Fear touched their faces. Even Sam Johnson, distaste in his eyes, looked the other way. Darrell Rumford had carved out a place for himself, deserved or not, and Fargo saw the man's sneering half-smile challenge him again.

"I'd like to see how fast you are, Fargo," Darrell Rumford said. "Because I'm the fastest damn draw you'll ever see."

"You telling me or yourself," Fargo asked mildly, and

saw Darrell Rumford's twisted smile disappear, his eyes grow smaller.

"I'm telling you," he growled.

"Thanks," Fargo said.

Doc Anderson cut in, nervousness in his voice. "I hope you'll stay around till you can meet the others, Fargo," he said. "They might feel well enough by the end of the day."

Fargo shrugged. "I can stay some," he said.

"Good, because some of us have discussed a few things we'd like to talk to you about," the doctor said. "Now I've my patients to check on again." He turned and went into his wagon and Fargo saw Darrell Rumford snap at his wife.

"Fix something to eat. I'm hungry," the man ordered. She went into the wagon with instant obedience and he followed, pushed her once because she took the tailgate step too slowly.

"Worm," he heard Karla Corrigan say as she glared at the closed door of the grocery wagon. She spun and disappeared into her own gray Studebaker farm wagon directly in front of him. Fargo saw Stacy Smith begin to walk back toward her baker's wagon at the end of the row.

"Forgetting something?" he called.

She halted, turned blue eyes on him that again carried cool arrogance in their questioning glance. "I don't believe so," she said. Fargo saw Bobby start to hurry away, head down. "Where are you going?" she called after him.

"Just around," Bobby tossed back as he kept walking.

"Stay close to the camp," Stacy admonished, turned her cool loveliness back to him. Against the neutral gray of Karla's farm wagon she was as striking as a jonquil in a bog. "You were saying?" she asked with polite coolness.

"Your offer, you seem to want to forget it," Fargo said.

47

A tiny furrow broke the smoothness of her forehead. "What offer?" she asked.

"The one you gave Bobby to carry," Fargo said.

The furrow deepened and he saw wariness come into the blue eyes. "What offer was that?" she slid out.

"Your offer that anyone who helped him get back could have you," Fargo said almost offhandedly, and watched her fine-lined lips drop open in a sharp gasp. "I have the feeling you're going back on that," he said.

Stacy Smith blinked at him, her lips still parted. "No, I'm not going back on that," she began.

"Good." Fargo smiled.

"I mean I never made it," she said quickly.

Fargo studied her. "You saying Bobby just made that up by himself?" he questioned.

"Indeed I am saying just that," Stacy Smith snapped, and her eyes peered across the hills. "Bobby Darrow, you come here," she called out, but nothing moved except a crow on a dead branch. She returned her eyes to Fargo, anger in their blue depths now. "How could you even believe such a thing?" she demanded.

Fargo shrugged. "You wouldn't be the first one to hold out that bait, honey," he said calmly.

"Well, I didn't hold out that bait, as you so crudely put it," she snapped.

"And you wouldn't be the first to pull the promise back after it worked," Fargo remarked, and watched fury color her face.

"Damn you, I'm not doing that, either. I never promised and I'm not pulling anything back," she almost screamed as his calm seemed to infuriate her more. "How can you believe anything else?" she flung out.

Fargo shrugged. "It got me here. That's all I really know," he said.

Icy disdain blazed from her eyes. "Are you saying that's the only reason you helped Bobby get back with the medicine?" she stabbed.

"It sweetened the pot," Fargo said calmly.

"You're impossible," Stacy Smith hissed. "And you'll not hold me to something I never offered."

"So you keep saying," Fargo returned.

"Dammit, I'll do more than that," Stacy hissed, whirled, stalked away from him, halted, and swept the nearby slope with her blazing eyes. "Bobby, you come down here," she called. "You come down here this minute or I'll see that you're tied up for the rest of the trip."

Fargo's eyes scanned the slope and he was first to see Bobby's head appear from behind a small escarpment of sandstone. Fargo leaned against the wagon and watched Bobby step fully into view, start down toward Stacy. She met him halfway, seized his arm, her face tight with fury. She half-flung him toward Fargo as she reached the wagons. "Now you tell the truth, damn you," she screamed at Bobby, and Fargo watched Bobby right himself, turn wide, round eyes on Stacy.

"But I did, Miss Stacy. I said just what you told me to say," the boy answered.

Fargo watched Stacy Smith's skin redden down to the base of her long, lovely neck and she trembled in rage. "Damn you, Bobby Darrow, you tell the truth," she shouted, her voice almost cracking.

But Bobby refused to be shaken, Fargo saw, his eyes staying wide with innocence. "Golly, Miss Stacy, you can change your mind. You don't have to get so mad about it," he said.

"I didn't change my mind and you know it," Stacy shot back, turned her eyes on Fargo. "He's simply lying. I never told him to say anything like that. He's a miserable little monster," she said.

"Somebody's lying, I'll admit that," Fargo commented.

"You want to believe him. That suits you just fine. Well, you can go ahead and believe whatever you damn please, but I'll be no part of it," the girl said. She speared Bobby with fury. "You'll pay for this, young man," she said. "You stay in camp until I've decided what to do with you."

She whirled and strode back to the baker's wagon, disappeared into it without a glance back, and Fargo saw the wagon shake as she stomped inside. He cast a glance at Bobby standing calmly beside him. "Let's ride some," he said, putting one foot in the pinto's stirrup.

"You heard what Miss Stacy said about me staying in camp," Bobby said, and sounded the soul of obedience.

"I'll take care of Miss Stacy," Fargo answered. "Get your horse." Bobby hurried away and Fargo slowly started up the slope past the red shale wall. Bobby caught up to him and the Trailsman rode close to where he'd spent the night, halted at a high glen where a layer of poverty grass formed a padding just thick enough to take the bone-breaking hardness from the ground. He dismounted, squatted down on his haunches as Bobby slid from his horse.

"I'm sorry about Miss Smith changing her mind," Bobby said. "But that's the way she is."

"Forget it." Fargo smiled and Bobby dropped to his knees, let himself gaze across the slope. He never saw the powerful arm that shot forward with the speed of a striking diamondback, but he felt it lift him, flip him up and into the air in a flailing somersault. Bobby crashed onto the circle of poverty grass with a bone-jarring thud, landing on his back. The breath went from him and his eyes glazed, and Fargo let him lay there for a moment. When the boy's eyes began to come back into focus, Fargo yanked him to a sitting position.

"Jeez," Bobby managed to gasp.

"Now you're going to tell the truth, you scheming little bastard," Fargo hissed. Bobby's eyes blinked, stared at the big man's angry face. "Stacy Smith never made that offer. Why'd you say she did?" Fargo said.

"You believing her?" Bobby tried, and Fargo lifted him half off the ground with one hand, shook him as though he were a rag doll.

"I don't have to believe her. I know, goddammit," Fargo roared. "The truth, damn you, or I'll break your little neck and say you fell off your horse."

Fargo saw fear swim into Bobby's eyes as he realized the threat was more than idle words. "I wanted you to come back with me," Bobby said, his voice suddenly small.

Fargo lowered him to the ground, kept his hand pulling the shirtfront into a knot under the small chin. "Why? Out with it," he growled.

"Because they'll never make it to California without somebody like you, not that bunch of fools," Bobby spat with surprising vehemence.

"And you want to get to California real bad," Fargo said.

"I sure do. I want to get there and get away from her," Bobby shot back.

There was no need to ask who "her" meant. "I got you back because of the medicine, not to take on a wagon train, especially one like this," Fargo said.

Bobby glowered. "You could stay on," he muttered. "Anyway, that's why I wanted you to come back with me."

"I don't favor somebody trying to trick me," Fargo said.

Bobby's glower remained. "How'd you know to believe her?" he asked.

"The minute I saw her," Fargo said. "She's not the kind to make that sort of offer. I knew you'd lied right then and there."

Bobby fell into brooding silence.

"What about the men who tried to get the medicine? What do you know about them?" Fargo asked.

"Nothing," Bobby said.

Fargo's arm shot out, his hand curling around the boy's neck. "No more games with me," he growled, his eyes peering at Bobby, taking in the flash of fear that came into the boy's face.

"I'm not lying. I don't know anything more about them than you do. Honest, Fargo," Bobby said. "I never saw them till they came after me."

Fargo drew his hand back, satisfied that Bobby was telling the truth, let his thoughts linger on the men that had come searching for their companions. They'd been cheated out of the medicine, but he still had the feeling that wouldn't end it. "I figure you all will be hearing from them again," he said, giving voice to his thoughts.

"You mean they'll come trying to get the medicine?" Bobby asked.

"Maybe. The medicine or something. I don't know. But you should tell the others they're likely to try again," Fargo said.

"Why don't you tell them?" Bobby answered instantly.

Fargo smiled. The boy continued to remain quick-witted, determined not to miss any opportunity. "You figure that'll help get me more involved." He chuckled. "No, thanks. They'll believe you." He rose, put one hand on the pinto's neck. "You go on down and tell them. I'll look around some."

"Why, if you're so all-fired set on not helping any?" Bobby answered sullenly.

"My own curiosity," Fargo said, the answer not an untruth. He swung up on the pinto, saw Bobby mount the quarterhorse.

"What'll I tell Miss Stacy?" Bobby muttered.

Fargo thought for a moment. "Tell her you decided to tell me the truth. That'll help your stock some," he answered.

"Thanks," Bobby muttered, but there was gratefulness in his voice.

Fargo watched him head down the slope and then turned the Ovaro and climbed higher. He rode leisurely and let his eyes move across the mountains. The Ruby Mountains were no steady upward progression but a series of ups and downs, rises and small valleys, ridges and hollows, shale and sandstone outcrops, plenty of mountain timber, most Sierra juniper, blue spruce, hawthorne, and Rocky Mountain maples. He made a wide, ragged half-circle around the place where the wagons were camped but staying above them on the high ground. His eyes sought motion, movement, a swaying of branches, a flash of unexpected color, the sudden upward dart of a kingbird, all the peripheral things that told him so much more.

He'd reached midway in the half-circle when he drew the pinto to a halt as, a dozen yards ahead and slightly below, three bronzed, near-naked horsemen stood side by side, unmoving, their backs to him. Their attention was directed downward into a hollow beyond his sight. He backed the Ovaro into a heavy-branched blue spruce until he was thoroughly hidden yet able to keep the three Indians in sight. They finally turned their ponies as one and moved silently, single-file, riding up into the mountains. One carried a pouch with beadwork on it. Nez Percé,

Fargo grunted, and waited till they were out of sight before moving from beneath the big spruce. He rode forward to where the Indians had halted and peered down into the hollow to see six men camped at the bottom of it. He spotted a narrow pathway in the trees at one side and moved the pinto downward toward the men. He had gone down close enough to hear voices when he halted, saw a seventh man appear on horseback at the other edge of the hollow. He rode into the camp, slid from the saddle, and took a tin mug near a battered white enamel coffeepot resting on hot coals.

"No signs they're going anywhere, not today," the man said.

Fargo saw a small, wiry figure in a black shirt and black pants detach himself from the others. He moved in quick steps, almost on the tip of his toes. He wasn't over five-four, Fargo guessed, a sharp face and near-white hair, and he paced up and down as he spoke.

"The kid, is he there?" the small man questioned.

"He's there, I saw him," the other man said as he started to drink his coffee.

"Shit. They got the medicine, then," the small figure said. His pacing increased in tempo and he seemed to be doing a strange little dance. "Goddamn, I sent enough of you out to stop that," he barked as he paced back and forth, each step almost a little dance.

"Christ, Maxey, Len and the others got themselves killed trying," the one man protested.

"They failed, that's why," Maxey said. The small man moved back and forth in front of the others not unlike a bantam rooster parading in front of his hens. "You just keep checking them out every few hours," he told the man who'd come back to the camp.

"That's stupid. They're not ready to move out. I told you that, Maxey," the man snapped back.

The little man called Maxey did a half-hopping whirl and Fargo saw the gun in his hand fire and the shot blow the other man's hat from his head.

"Sure thing, Maxey, sure thing," the man shouted as he dropped to the ground. Maxey lowered his gun into its holster and with quick, prancing steps, moved to the side of the camp, folded his small figure onto the ground. The little man was quick, Fargo noted, quick with his feet and with his hands.

Fargo waited, watched the camp settle down to silent waiting, and he backed the pinto between two spruces, turned the horse around, and retraced steps back up to the top of the slope. He rode on, completed the last of the half-circle, and began to move downward to where the wagons were camped. It was late in the day when he reached the scene, saw Karla Corrigan pounding a handful of clothes against a rock to squeeze the last water from them. Darrell Rumford sat at the tailgate of his green grocery wagon, his face set sullenly. Sam Johnson lay half under his wagon working on one of the fellies of the right rear wheel.

As he dismounted, Fargo saw Doc Anderson hurry toward him, and out of the corner of his eye he glimpsed Stacy Smith stepping from her wagon, starting toward him.

"Glad you're back," the doctor said. "The others are feeling well enough to meet you." He led the way toward the big dray with the canvas wrapped around its stake sides, rapped on the wood edge of the wagon frame. A woman stepped out of the rear of the wagon in moments, about fifty years of age, Fargo guessed, a big woman with flat breasts who had abandoned a waistline long ago.

"Mildred Rogers, Fargo," the doctor introduced.

The woman nodded and Fargo saw that she had a pinched face that seemed out of place on her big frame, a thin mouth, and a pale complexion he attributed to having been ill. The man who followed her from the big dray seemed small in comparison to the woman, but his mouth echoed her pinched-in face. "Dan Rogers," Doc Anderson said. Dan Rogers wore his remaining hair slicked sideways and flat across his skull in an effort to make less do more.

"The doc told us how we all owe you," Mildred Rogers said, and offered a somewhat bloodless smile.

"Saved Mildred, you did," the man chimed in. "She was real bad till the doc got those injections into her."

Fargo nodded. "You can thank Bobby. If it weren't for Bobby, I'd have never come into the picture. He got the medicine in the first place," Fargo said. "Nobody seems to remember that."

Out of the corner of his eye he saw Stacy Smith's face tighten, her eyes frost over as she listened.

"No, we're not forgetting about Bobby. He did the job for us, all right," Dan Rogers added with almost apologetic haste.

Fargo felt Doc Anderson's touch at his elbow. "Over here, please. I want you to meet Harlan Billings," the man said. Following, Fargo saw the trio of figures that had emerged from the big Conestoga, the center one a man in a royal-blue silk dressing gown that couldn't hide the folds of flesh around his middle. Fargo took in a round face that seemed to be made of hanging jowls and a large, fleshy nose on which little eyes seemed to perch as though they'd been stuck there with glue. The two figures that flanked him were younger, both tall and thin-framed, faces that were tanned yet somehow seemed pallid. The two men were not twins yet gave the impression that they might be, reinforced by the look of sullenness on both their faces, their hands on their holsters in a truculent stance. "Mr. Billings, this is Fargo," Doc Anderson introduced. "These are Billings' nephews, Zeke and Zach."

"Harlan Billings," the hanging jowls said, the tiny eyes seeming to smile. "Glad to make your acquaintance. I think you are owed a reward."

"You want to reward somebody, reward Bobby," Fargo said.

"A boy doesn't need money," Harlan Billings said. "But we've another offer for you."

The doctor's voice cut in. "It's what we want to talk to you about," he said, and Fargo saw the others halt their activities and move in closer. Darrell Rumford rose, stepped forward, and Emmy came out of the grocery wagon, followed with tentative steps. She had a white cotton blouse on, given faint shape only by the two tiny high mounds. He saw her eyes meet his for an instant and turn away. Doc Anderson's voice brought his attention back to the man. "Bobby told us about those men and how you think they might attack us for the medicine," the physician said.

"For something," Fargo commented.

"If not for the medicine, what, then?" Doc Anderson asked, and Fargo shrugged. "No matter, they pose a threat. Everything out there does. We want you to stay on and take us through to Amagosa. We'll pay you top dollar. We'll chip in to do so."

Fargo's eyes moved across the group. Darrell Rumford's face remained angry and Stacy's eyes hadn't lost their frost. The others waited anxiously.

"Why'd you decide you need somebody?" Fargo asked.

"It's become clear to us that we don't have the knowledge to make the journey on our own," the doctor answered. "We started out thinking we could. We were wrong."

Harlan Billings interjected. "I'm a man of means. I

should have hired someone such as yourself to take me through alone. I should never have entrusted my welfare to this pack of incompetents," he boomed out.

"But you did," Fargo said. "You must've had a reason."

"A mistake in judgment. I thought there'd be safety in numbers," the man answered.

Fargo's glance swept the others again. "Everybody agree to this?" he questioned.

"I'm going along with it only because it was that or quit the train," Darrell Rumford said. "So far as I'm concerned we can make it on our own. I could get us through."

"Anybody else?" Fargo asked. No one spoke and he paused at Stacy Smith to see only faint acceptance in the coolness of her face.

"If I take you through, you do exactly what I say, when I say, and how I say," Fargo told them. "I'm not here to debate anything."

"You'll be in charge. We've agreed to that," the doctor said.

"I don't do anything I don't want to do, Fargo," Darrell Rumford said. "And don't push me 'less you want to really see how fast I can draw."

"No need for that," Fargo said calmly. "I figure a fast gun is valuable on a trip like this." It was a turn-away answer and he saw Darrell Rumford's arrogant face accept it as a sign of weakness, a small victory. Fargo let him hold the thought. There'd be time for facing off Rumford if it had to come.

"Well, Fargo?" he heard Harlan Billings rumble, and he met the frown over the little flesh-enclosed eyes.

"I'll think on it till morning," Fargo said.

The man leaned over and the blue silk dressing gown fell open to reveal the thick, fatty pectorals and the bulging curve of his stomach. "Hell, you've come all this

58

way. You might as well turn a good dollar for it," Billings said.

"I'll be considering that," Fargo said.

"We can be quite certain of that much," Stacy Smith cut in, her voice coated with disdain.

"That doesn't sit right with you?" Fargo asked.

"I'd prefer being led by someone who didn't always require a reward of one kind or another, someone who cared about helping," she said loftily.

"You want a trailsman or a preacher?" Fargo rasped. "You pay me for knowing, not caring." His eyes flicked across at the others, caught Karla Corrigan's amused observation. "I'll tell you come morning," he said again, and the others began to turn away. He returned his eyes to Stacy. "Bobby talk to you?" he asked.

"Yes," she said. "You should never have believed him in the first place."

"No reason not to," Fargo said mildly. "Seems to me you still owe me."

Her frown was instant. "How can you possibly think that?" she snapped.

"You're responsible for him, for what he does and what he says," Fargo answered.

"Oh, you'd like that, wouldn't you? It'd suit you just fine to have me take that position," Stacy returned.

"You can take any position you like, honey." Fargo grinned.

Stacy glared at him, her fine-lined lips pressed hard on each other, and she whirled, stalked away in angry disgust. He was getting to know just how her little rear moved, Fargo reflected. From a distance, he grunted, a situation that would change in time if he decided to stay on. He started toward his pinto as the dusk slid over the camp, paused as Doc Anderson came toward him. "I hope you'll take us on, Fargo," the man said. "I'm worried. I'd say everyone will be well enough to travel with one day more of rest and the last round of injections. But we need experienced leadership."

"Is that the only reason you're worried?" Fargo asked.

"I'm worried about not getting to California," the man said. "It's very important to me that I get there."

"I'd guess it's important to everybody in this train," Fargo answered.

"Some have more important reasons than others," the man said, and his tired face seemed to take on added tiredness. He walked away, shoulders slumped, and Fargo watched him go, started to mount the pinto when he saw Bobby appear out of the twilight. The boy's face held a note of uncertain truculence.

"Now what's eating you, boy?" Fargo said. "Stacy Smith sitting too hard on you?"

"No," Bobby muttered, looked up at the big man from under his brows. "I'm just surprised."

"At what?" Fargo asked.

"You being afraid of Darrell Rumford like everybody else around here," Bobby said.

"Is that what you think?" Fargo asked.

"You backed off from him again," Bobby glowered.

"Guess you'll have to stay surprised, then," Fargo said as he pulled himself onto the pinto. He touched the horse with his knee and the animal started to move forward.

"Fargo," Bobby called, "I didn't mean that. I know you're not afraid of him."

Fargo paused to look back at the boy, his lake-blue eyes hard. "No, you don't," he said, and rode on.

Bobby desperately wanted to look up to someone, to believe in somebody. But he was picking out the wrong things to worship, the same wrong things too many grown men picked out. There'd be no good done for the boy by playing into those reasons. Bobby had to learn that the measure of a man wasn't made of how fast he could shoot.

Fargo spurred the Ovaro forward, up the sharp slope to where he'd bedded down before as the night wrapped itself around the land. Reaching the spot, he dismounted and laid out his bedroll, stripped down to his trousers, munched on some cold beef jerky, and relaxed in the warm night to watch the half-moon float its way across the sky.

He let his thoughts drift, first to the men that waited and watched higher on the mountain. They'd wanted the medicine once, but it was unimportant now. That proved they'd only wanted it as a weapon of some sort and now they had to plan something else. His thoughts went to the offer that had been made to him. Any wagon train could run into trouble. Trouble was a commodity to be expected on the trail. Yet some outfits had trouble built into them; this one not only had it built in but it was already waiting in the wings.

He grimaced. Yet they were as sheep going to the slaughter if left on their own. Darrell Rumford was a blowhard, he was convinced. Doc Anderson was a hollow shell, the others all followers. Only Stacy Smith had steel enough in her to lead, but that was all she had, no experience, no common sense, no understanding of people or places.

Fargo grimaced again. Top dollar was always inviting, but not if it meant your neck for sure. His thoughts broke off as he caught the sound, the jangle of rein chains, the sound of a horse blowing air through its nostrils. He rose to one knee, the Colt instantly in his hand, peered down the slope, and found the dark shape of a horse and rider moving tentatively, uncertainly.

"Fargo," he heard the voice call, and his brows lifted in surprise. He rose, dropped the gun into its holster.

"Up here," he called, and watched the horse turn, make its way up to the small ledge. "Wasn't expecting visitors," he said as Karla Corrigan slid from her horse, turned to face him. The moonlight glinted on the black hair on one side. "Something on your mind?"

"Definitely." Karla smiled. "Heard you and Stacy outside my wagon. I thought you had a point. So Bobby lied. You're still owed something. But you knew she wasn't going to see it that way."

"No harm in trying," Fargo said.

"So I figured I'd make it up to you," Karla said, the amusement in her eyes. He watched her fingers at the top button of her shirt, saw her flip the button open.

"You telling me you've come to be a sort of stand-in?" Fargo asked.

"More like a lay-in," Karla answered, her laugh low and warm.

"Yes, that'd be more accurate." Fargo nodded.

"I figured you to be a man who likes accuracy," Karla said as her fingers undid the next two buttons of her shirt. "After all, you were lured here under false pretenses, you might say."

"No doubt about it," he agreed happily.

"Stacy Smith isn't going to make it up to you, not that stiff-backed bitch," Karla said.

The thought came at once, but he held it inside himself. Not yet, but she'll make it up in time, he vowed silently. "You're right," he answered aloud to Karla, and watched her undo the remaining few buttons of the shirt. The garment fell open and her breasts surged forward as if with an eagerness of their own to show their full, round beauty.

Fargo's hand pushed the blouse back, slid it from Karla Corrigan's shoulders. The twin mounds were modest but beautifully turned, undersides filling with perfect, symmetrical curves, a buttermilk softness with dusty-pink tips.

Karla dropped to her knees on the bedroll, waited, her eyes staying on the muscled leanness of his torso, the magnificent contours of his shoulders and pectorals. He undid his trousers, let them fall to the ground, and the maleness of him had already responded to her waiting loveliness, thrust itself out of his shorts with its own eager pride, and he heard Karla's quick gasp of breath. He dropped down beside her, pulled at her skirt, and it came off in his hands at once. She had good hips, her abdomen almost flat, just enough of a curve to it to offer soft promise. Nice legs, perhaps a trifle thin, yet with long, slow curves, opened from below a dark triangle as modest as her breasts, yet attractive. His hand reached forward, touched, no wiry harshness but a soft almost silky quality. He drew his hand up through the soft nap, his palm pressing against her abdomen, moved up across her stomach, and he sank to his knees beside her. She fell back on the bedroll and his mouth found one buttermilk soft breast, closed around its dusty-pink tip.

"Oh, Jesus," Karla gasped out, and he felt her hands reaching for him, finding his hardness against her, closing her fingers around him. "Oh, God, Jesus . . . Oh, God," she murmured.

His tongue caressed the dusty-pink tip of her breast, brushing over it with warm wetness, and he heard her half-cry, felt her body twist, half-turn, come back again to press against him. Her hand around his maleness pulled him toward her and he felt her legs falling open.

"Please, quick, oh, please," she gasped out. "Yes, oh, God, yes, now, oh, please, please." Her legs were opened wide, quivering, and he felt her pulling on him, guiding, demanding. She began to quiver and he let her take him inside her, pressed his throbbing warmth forward. Karla screamed, her voice rising, changing to a moan, then rising again. She was shaking, her hands clutching feverishly at him. In surprise, he felt her pushing hard, quivering, already on her way to that singular summit.

"Please, please, please," she gasped, and he pushed forward with her, felt her stiffen, her back arch, and the scream erupted from her lips as her pelvis trembled against him. "Aaaaaaiiiiiiii, oh, aaaiiiiii," she wailed as she erupted, and her hands became fists that pounded against the bedroll until suddenly she gave a sharp shudder and fell back on the ground.

Her arms came up to encircle his neck as Fargo stayed inside her, filling the warm glove with quietude, and he saw her eyes come open, look up at him. A slow smile touched her lips. "Now make love to me," she murmured. "Start over."

He drew back slowly, slipped from her, and she gave a small cry of discordance but drew her legs up, held them together primly, and half-turned, offered her breasts to his mouth. Fargo pulled gently on each, caressing their softness with lips, tongue, fastening his lips on the dusty-pink nipples and drawing them upward.

"Aaaah . . . ah . . . ah," Karla murmured, and he felt her body against him moving slowly up and down, rubbing herself against his pulsating firmness. No instant trembling now, no headlong quivering, but a slow, snakelike motion of her entire body, and she lifted her arms from around him, slid her breast from his mouth, moved down along his hard-muscled frame with her lips. "Aiiieee . . . oh, Jesus," he heard her gasp as she found him, held him to her, drew him into her lips. "Oh, yes, yes . . . oh,

God almighty," Karla muttered, and then pulled away, half-rolled, legs moving open to welcome him. "Please, Fargo," he heard her say, no terrible demand in it this time but a breathy cry of desire.

He let his hand move through the soft triangle, found her wet lips opened, and her little half-scream was instant at his touch. He caressed her, drawing a slow circle around her soft moistness, and her gasps became low, throaty sounds, almost groans. He moved, came atop her, rested the tip of his pulsating organ on the edge of her.

"Oh, oh, ooooooh, please, please," she groaned, pressed upward to take him in, and he let himself slowly move into her. Her hands came down on the bedroll with a sudden snap as she thrust upward to encompass all of him, and there were no words now, only soft groaning sounds.

Karla moved with him in undulant motions, her legs coming up to lock around his back, the vise of eternal pleasure, and he could feel her calf muscles work against him as she pushed him deeper into her. She lifted her head, wrapped arms around his neck, and pressed her mouth on his, pushing her tongue forward in rhythm with his every slow push inside her, sensual echoes of the flesh, passion's mimicry. He felt his own surgings begin, quickened his pace, and she stayed in rhythm with him until there was no time left for echoes. The reality of desire soared, its own master now, and he felt himself explode inside her, felt her answering tightness, and her cry came against his neck, a long, wavering call, her teeth pressing into his skin until finally the long cry ended in a rush of breathy murmurings. "Fargo, oh, God, Fargo . . . wonderful . . . so wonderful . . . aaah . . . aaah." The murmurings trailed off to tiny sighs and her teeth pulled from his neck as she lay on her back, drawing in quick little breaths. He let himself enjoy the buttermilk softness of her curves and

65

contours. Her eyes, half-closed, came open fully and the slow smile he'd come to know slid over her lips.

"You were in a hell of a hurry at first," Fargo commented.

"It's that way with me sometimes," she said.

"You've been away from the well a long time," he said.

Karla's smile broadened reflectively. "Too long," she said. "When you came into camp I knew waiting was over for me."

"So you didn't come here just to make it up to me." He grinned, and she half-shrugged.

"That was part of it," she said.

"What else was part of it? Convincing me to stay on?" he asked.

"No," Karla answered at once. "I know better. That wouldn't be enough to sway you."

Fargo lay down beside her and she half-turned to rest against him. "Tell me about Karla Corrigan," Fargo said. "That'll help me make up my mind."

"Knowing about me?" She frowned.

"You and everyone else," Fargo told her.

She rose onto one elbow and one dusty-pink tip brushed against his chest. "Why is that important?" she questioned.

"I take on a train, I want to know what I've got. It helps when the going gets rough," he said. He said nothing about the men waiting higher in the hills. They were too much a question mark yet. "Let's get back to Karla Corrigan," Fargo said, brushing one nipple with his lips before pulling back to listen. "Why is she part of this train?"

"I've a man waiting for me in California, Tom Jarrell," she said. She put her arms behind her head and her breasts rose up in sheer loveliness. "He's twenty-five years older than I am, but he's made his money and he wants to marry me. I've been around long enough to know that a good man is hard to find, and Tom's a good man."

"Loving him isn't part of it, I take it," Fargo said.

"He loves me and that's enough for me to make a go of it. I like him. I'm comfortable with him. Maybe the rest will come later," Karla said. "I've worked hard at being faithful to him for almost a year. He's been out there getting settled for that long." The smile that came to her lips was suddenly rueful, full of self-amusement. "Did pretty good at it until you rode into camp with Bobby," she said. "I decided then that faithful was one thing and being a damn fool another." She reached both arms up, circled his neck. "Does that tell you enough about Karla Corrigan?" she asked, the cool amusement back in her eyes.

"For now," he said.

Her mouth lifted, took his, opened, her tongue caressing, and she pulled him down onto the bedroll with her, her hands reaching along his ribs, across his hard abdomen. When she found him, he was rising for her, his eagerness matching her wanting.

The moon was high in the night sky when her final scream curled through the darkness and she lay hard against him until breath returned. She half-slept for a spell and then rose, began to dress as he watched her. Finished, she turned to him, blew a kiss with her lips, and climbed onto her horse. He watched her disappear down the slope and lay back, a little smile edging his lips. The night had become one of unexpected surprises. Maybe, despite her denial, she hoped the night would help him make up his mind to stay. He smiled broadly. It hadn't hurt any, he murmured as he closed his eyes and slept.

4

When morning came, he dressed leisurely, gave the camp time to wake before he slowly started down the slope. He'd gone halfway when his ears caught the soft splash of water behind a stand of blue spruce. He turned the pinto, made his way silently through the trees to halt when he came in sight of a little mountain pool bubbling up from an underground spring in the center. As he watched, the girl rose up from beneath the water, shaking soap from her dark-blond hair. Fargo stayed immobile as Stacy Smith leaned backward, did a back flip into the water, and came up, hair rinsed thoroughly now. She rose on underwater footing, straightened up, half out of the water, and the morning sun highlighted the tiny drops of water that covered her naked beauty.

She turned toward him, stretched, and Fargo watched long breasts lift, well-rounded undersides and tiny pale-pink nipples—virginal breasts, yet womanly enough to be exciting. Stacy's waist narrowed quickly into equally narrow hips that edged a flat abdomen. She began to walk from the pool and he saw long legs, beautifully shaped, smooth, long thighs without a mark, vein, or blemish, and a bushy little triangle, dark and dense even wet down as it was now. She halted beside a rock where her clothes lay, stretched again, and he felt his breath draw in at the beauty of her. She complemented the little mountain pool and the blue spruce, holding the same pure, cool beauty in her, something untouched and pristine about her. She half-spun one way, then the other, and little droplets of water spun from her body, each tiny drop caught by the new sun. She folded herself down on the grass beside the rock, let the sun dry her long, willowy body.

Fargo backed the pinto silently from the trees and turned, continued his way down to the wagons. He saw Bobby playing tag with the two Johnson girls, Doc Johnson sipping coffee from a small tin cup beside a tiny fire. Karla, hanging clothes at the tailgate of her wagon, looked up as he rode into the camp, and he caught the quick amusement in her glance. Fargo saw Emmy Rumford filling a wooden tub of water from one of the casks at the back of the grocery wagon. He dismounted beside her. Wearing the same long, gray dress, she glanced up and her cheekbone bore a red welt, unmistakably the result of a blow. She saw his eyes linger on the bruise and she straightened up, took hold of the tub, and her chin lifted almost defiantly. Her eyes met his and asked for no sympathy.

"He feeling especially nasty last night?" Fargo asked.

"No more than usual," she said, her voice a monotone. She took her eyes away from his and the cowed air flooded her face at once.

"Ever look for a way out?" Fargo asked quietly.

She didn't glance up. "Maybe," she said, started to lift the tub when Darrell Rumford's head burst from the rear of the wagon.

"Where the hell's the water?" he shouted, halted when he saw Fargo beside Emmy. He stepped from the wagon, bare-chested, a well-muscled body, and the cruelly arrogant smile twisted his mouth. "Passing the time of day with the mighty Trailsman," he said with heavy sarcasm to Emmy as she started past him. "You wouldn't be his type. He don't like the mousy kind." The man laughed. Emmy went into the wagon and Fargo found it took more effort to keep the calmness in his face.

"Why are you with the train?" he asked the younger man.

"What the hell's that your business?" Rumford snapped.

"I take this train, everything about it is my business," Fargo said. "I want an answer or you're out, mister," he added, unable to keep the edge from coming into his voice.

Darrell Rumford's mouth held its twisted arrogance. "You're just looking for trouble, aren't you, big man?" he said, and his eyes flicked to make sure the others were watching.

"I'm looking for answers," Fargo said calmly.

Darrell Rumford let an air of expansiveness come over him. "What the hell, it's no matter to me. There's time yet for you and me," he said.

"So there is," Fargo agreed quietly. "Now, why are you heading California way?"

"I got itchy feet. I don't like to stay too long in one place," Rumford said. "I thought I'd give California a try."

Fargo saw Emmy appear at the door of the wagon, listening. Her pinched little face showed nothing, yet her eyes were fastened on Darrell Rumford; and Fargo caught something in them, as though, for an instant, she was about to contradict him. But she turned back into the wagon, eyes downcast. Fargo turned from Darrell Rumford and halted beside the doctor.

"My brother practices medicine in Amagosa. We're both

70

getting on in years. I want to see him one more time before it's too late, maybe set up a joint practice out there with him," the physician said.

Fargo nodded, turned away to see Harlan Billings had emerged from the big Conestoga, flanked once again by his two sullen-faced nephews. The man still wore the blue silk dressing gown, but now he had donned trousers under it, Fargo noted.

"Heard you talking to Rumford," Harlan Billings rumbled. "I've important business deals waiting for me in California. It's vital I get there as quickly as possible. I'm no idle wanderer or farmer looking for a place to light. I'm an important man."

"You be sure and tell that to the Shoshoni if they come looking." Fargo smiled. He walked on to where Kate Johnson stood holding her husband's arm. "I'll take a guess for you, Sam. Homesteading?" Fargo said.

The man nodded. "Nothing went right for us up in Idaho. We figured California might be a new start," he said.

"Might be," Fargo said as he went on to halt before Dan and Mildred Rogers, the question in his eyes.

"Always wanted to retire out in California," the man said, trying to make his pinched-in face appear genial.

Fargo's eyes went to his wife and he saw Mildred smile back, but her tongue licked nervously at her lips.

"Dan's worked hard. It's time he retired and enjoyed life. We both decided on California," she said. Again, Fargo caught the nervous twitch of her mouth, her pinched-in smile too full of effort.

"I hope you both make it," he grunted, started toward the last wagon. It was, with its sliding door and drop windows and neat, boxy shape, as prim as the owner, he reflected. Stacy, in her yellow shirt and black skirt, stood

71

beside the wagon as Bobby stomped away, his face wreathed in darkness.

"Mr. Johnson didn't mind," Fargo heard the boy toss back.

"I don't care. Those are my orders," Stacy called after the small form, her tone made of severity.

"Still bearing down on the kid?" Fargo asked mildly.

Cool disdain colored her eyes as she turned to him. "I'll not have him going off alone with the Johnson girls," she said.

"Why not, especially as Mr. Johnson doesn't mind?" Fargo queried.

"You know very well why not," Stacy said icily.

"He's at the age for exploring and experimenting. So are the girls. You can't hold back nature," Fargo said.

"Nonsense," she snapped.

"I forgot, you've had a lot of practice holding back," he remarked.

The frost formed in her eyes. "And you have obviously made a career of not holding anything back," she speared, and was plainly pleased with her return.

"Fair enough." Fargo laughed. "But you're still handling Bobby the wrong way."

"He's a little monster. You don't know," she said. "I've tried to know the boy."

"With what?" Fargo shot back, and saw her frown. "To know you've got to be able to feel. Kids and dogs, they feel, they sense, they pick up things. They know from inside."

"And I don't?" she questioned.

"Honey, all you know is holding back," Fargo said.

Fury pushed the cool disdain from her eyes. "How dare you?" she threw at him. "You've only just met me a day ago. You don't know anything about me."

"I don't have to bite a peach to tell when it's not ripe," Fargo answered.

Her lips tightened against each other, yet stayed fine-lined, a sensitive mouth even compressed in anger, he noted. "I can do without more of your saddle wisdom," she said tartly. "You didn't stop by just to talk about Bobby, I'm sure."

"Came to find out how you hooked up with this train," Fargo said. "Bobby told me you're taking him to relatives at the foot of the Amagosa range."

"That's right," Stacy said. "Bobby's parents were killed in a fire up in Balanced Rock, Idaho Territory. Friends of the parents took him in, but he was too wild. He kept running away and getting into trouble. Judge Wilson put him in the sheriff's custody and I was made his guardian."

"Why you?" Fargo cut in.

"Because I was experienced. I worked in a home for orphans," Stacy replied. "His aunt and uncle were reached in California, but it took six months. They agreed to take him, finally, and I'm bringing him there."

"Courtesy of the sheriff's office," Fargo said.

"That's right." She nodded. "Anything else you feel you must know?" The disdain had returned to her eyes.

"Not for now," Fargo said, paused, saw her eyes still on him. "There is one thing. No more going off to mountain pools alone," he said, and saw her lips part, the blue eyes grow round. A faint tinge of color began to appear in her cheeks. "Very nice indeed, but you don't want some big buck taking you back to his tepee all wet and naked, do you?" Fargo smiled, and her faint tinge of color became a rush of pink.

"Have you no manners at all, no sense of decency?" she accused.

"Sure I have. I didn't interrupt you, did I?" Fargo

grinned as he strode away. He heard her breath escaping in a hiss of fury as he continued walking toward the center of the camp.

Doc Anderson was in the open, near the small fire, and he saw the others moving from their wagons. They'd each given him their stories, for what they were worth, he mused silently. But he'd accept each one for now, he had decided, and he halted before Doc Anderson as the others gathered closer.

"I'll take you as far as you can go," he said. "That won't be far for some of you who got wagons that won't hold up."

"Good, good," Doc Anderson said. "We've your pay already collected. Half now, half when we're there."

Fargo nodded agreement. "We'll take the Scully wagon. It'll come in handy. Some of you clean it out and get it ready to roll," he said, and his eyes paused at Harlan Billings and his two nephews. "I saw plenty of grouse, mountain quail, wild turkey, and rabbit. Zeke, Zach, and you, Rumford, go out and bag as many as you can and bring them back by afternoon."

"I'm no errand boy. Get somebody else," Darrell Rumford growled.

"I thought you were good with a gun," Fargo said mildly. It wasn't time to challenge Darrell Rumford.

"That doesn't mean I'm going chicken-shooting," Rumford snapped.

Fargo stayed calm, half-shrugged. "I thought it was something you'd enjoy. Sam Johnson can go," he said.

Darrell Rumford stepped forward, a braggart's magnanimity in his tone. "Shit, I'll do it. I'll hit what I aim at," he said.

Fargo nodded. Rumford had done his thing before everyone without drawing a direct challenge. He was satisfied.

Fargo let it stay that way and turned to Karla and Kate Johnson.

"When the birds are brought in, I want them cleaned and cooked, every one of them," he said.

"Why?" Karla frowned.

"I want cooked meat, ready just to warm and eat, no long campfire roasting for the next few days," Fargo told her.

"We'll be ready to move out in the morning," Doc Anderson said.

Fargo fastened a hard glance on the man. "You'll be ready to move out at midnight," he said, turned, and led the pinto away, the surprise still hanging in their faces. He walked slowly, casually, with the magnificent horse nudging his back. There were other eyes watching the camp, he was certain. The little man Maxey had ordered someone to keep watch, and up in the surrounding hills, a figure crouched, waited, observed. He would see the trio leave to hunt, watch them return with the catch. He'd wonder, frown in confusion at first, then hopefully reach certain conclusions.

Fargo glanced back to watch Rumford and the other two men leave the camp, each with rifle in hand. He moved on, had gone another half-dozen yards, halted to mount the pinto when he heard the shouts erupt, angry, high-pitched voices. He turned, saw Bobby with Abby Johnson, both standing face to face, screaming at each other.

"He's not afraid of Darrell Rumford, he's not," Fargo heard Bobby shout.

"He is, he is," the girl shouted back, and suddenly words became actions as Bobby seized her by the shoulders and shook her as he screamed.

"No, he's not, he's not, dammit," Bobby shouted.

Abby slapped his face, kicked out, and Bobby let go of

her to grab at his knee in pain. In seconds they were rolling on the ground, hitting and pulling at each other as they shouted half in tears. Fargo reached them in three long strides before Sam Johnson did. He bent over, pulled them apart, yanked them both to their feet, one in each big hand.

"That's enough, goddammit," he roared.

"She started it. She said you were scared," Bobby shouted back between gulps of breath.

"I heard what Abby said," Fargo interrupted, his face set as he turned a hard glance at the girl.

"Well, it sure looks like it," Abby Johnson said with truculent boldness.

Sam Johnson's voice cut in. "That'll be enough out of you, young lady," the man said, and closed a hand around his daughter's arm. He dragged the girl away as she fell silent, her face still truculent.

Fargo lifted Bobby, almost threw him onto the pinto, and swung up into the saddle behind him. He cantered from the camp, glimpsed Stacy Smith looking after him. Halting behind a line of blue spruce, he dismounted, waited while Bobby got down from the horse. His eyes were hard blue as they bored into Bobby, saw a mixture of remorse and defiance in the boy's face.

"You figure I ought to thank you for standing up for me?" Fargo asked.

"Sort of," Bobby answered with defiance edging his voice. "What's wrong with that?"

"What's wrong is your idea of what makes a man," Fargo said, and the boy stared back with his face set tight. "You think Darrell Rumford's a man?" Fargo prodded.

"No," Bobby snapped in disgust. "He's nothing but a big bully, always hittin' his wife and lording it over everybody."

"What if he's a real fast draw?" Fargo questioned. "What if he can outdraw me? Would that make him any better person? Would that make him a man?" He waited and Bobby looked away, his lips pressed together, frowning as the core of the question dug at him. "Spoiling for a fight doesn't make a man, either. And trying to avoid one doesn't make a coward." Bobby remained silent, stared at the ground. "Now you go back and think about those things," Fargo said. "Think hard about them, boy."

Bobby started to turn away, paused to look up at the big man, and Fargo saw the need leap into the boy's eyes, hope and wanting and all his inner conflicts mixed together in the quick glance. "You're not afraid of him, are you, Fargo?" Bobby asked, and Fargo grimaced inwardly. The boy's need to believe in someone or something remained deep. Channeling it the right way was one thing. Stomping on it wouldn't help.

Fargo drew a deep breath as he chose words. "No, I'm not afraid of him, but that's not what matters," he said. "You just think about what I told you."

"Yes, sir," Bobby said, hurried away, confidence restored in his quick glance, and Fargo drew another sigh as he swung onto the pinto. Bobby was a mixture: grown-up shrewdness and little-boy needs. Stacy Smith was right in one thing. He was a handful and she was no match for him. Not till she did her own growing up, he grunted as he sent the pinto upward into the trees, disappeared into thick cover.

He rode east, upward, not hurrying, staying in tree cover. He heard the sound of the others' shooting game until it faded away and he moved along the high ground. He rode the half-circle along the top of the nearest hills and let the day wear on. It was late afternoon when he reached the passage that led down to where the men had camped. He rode slowly downward, dismounted when he drew near, and went forward on foot until he dropped to one knee and let his eyes scan the scene in front of him.

The little man, Maxey, still paced the length of the camp in his all-black outfit, interspersing a little skipping step every few feet. Maxey had a nervous tick of some kind, Fargo decided, and he wondered if the little man ever stopped pacing. He let his eyes travel over the others as they lounged on the ground at the perimeter of the site and suddenly Maxey stopped pacing, fastened one of the men with a sharp glare. "They've been cooking and roasting birds?" He frowned.

"That's right," the man said, a sharp-faced figure with little eyes. "They ain't going anywhere, I tell you. They're fixing to have themselves a feast."

"Why?" Maxey spit out, and continued his quick little steps back and forth.

The man shrugged. "Most of them been sick. I figure they got to get some food into themselves," he said.

The little man paused in his pacing again, frowned at the other man. "Probably," he muttered. "You're probably right. But you get down there come morning and you keep your eye on them."

"Don't worry, they ain't ready to leave yet," the sharp-faced one said.

Fargo drew back, and a thin smile touched his mouth. He had guessed right. The oaf hadn't disappointed him, the man's conclusions simple and stolid. He rose, backed silently from his vantage spot, and returned to the pinto. A furrow pressed his forehead as he slowly rode back to the high ground. The band of men wanted the wagon train watched, wanted to be sure where it was at all times. Yet they'd made no move to attack. Why not? he wondered. What kept them nervously watching and waiting? The question offered no answer for itself and he pushed it aside for the moment.

The night had fallen around him when he rode into camp to see three fires still burning. Kate Johnson tended one, Karla another, and Stacy Smith and Emmy at the third. "This is the last of it," Karla said. "They ought to be done in a few minutes."

Fargo nodded approval. "Pack them with the others," he said, and sat down. Karla brought a tin plate of grouse, still warm, and beans. She paused beside him as he ate, the cool amusement playing around her lips again.

"Moving out at midnight sort of ruins some plans I'd held," she murmured.

"Guess so," Fargo said.

"I can wait." Karla laughed and returned to the fire.

Fargo watched Emmy take the bird from the wooden spit. She worked silently, the cowed air a part of everything she did. And then her eyes flicked to him, a brief instant, and he saw the flash of dark anger concealed in their depths. She glanced away at once, her attention on her task.

Fargo rose, spoke softly, but his voice carried across the campsite. "Finish up and get some sleep. You'll have almost four hours for it," he said. He walked to a far corner by himself, rested his back against a flat rock, and closed his eyes to sleep in moments, getting the most out of the first hours of deep sleep. The moon was in the midnight sky when he woke and he waited, let the others begin to emerge from their wagons. Doc Anderson was first, his tired face seeming more haggard than usual.

"It's the men up there, isn't it?" he asked. "That's why we're pulling out at this ungodly hour."

Fargo nodded. "We'll roll through the night and sleep in the day."

"But they'll pick up the wagon tracks easily enough," the man said.

"Yes, but I figure it'll still give us about eight hours head start," Fargo said. "If we can do the same thing for another night or two, we'll be out in the open where I want to be." He turned as the others came near. "Hitch the Scullys' wagon behind the Conestoga," he said.

"There are a few things we left inside it, a trunk, a small desk, some pillows, and a mattress," Karla told him. "We figured they might come in handy."

Fargo shrugged. "I'd rather have it empty, but leave it for now," he said. "We'll move slow to start—the slower, the less noise. They're too high up to hear us, unless we try rolling fast." He waited as the others turned into their wagons, moved up to the front, where Stacy held the reins. She wore a dark-green shirt that rested lightly to outline the long, graceful shape of her breasts, and he found himself remembering her glistening loveliness at the pool. He raised his arm, brought it forward, and Stacy snapped the reins to move their baker's wagon off at the head of the train. Fargo saw Bobby poke his head from one of the drop windows, fighting off sleep to watch the caravan move.

Fargo rode out in front of Stacy and kept the pace almost at a crawl as they began to roll downward. He let the pace pick up only when they'd reached the next level and swung onto a narrow, fairly flat passage between lichen-covered shale formations. A narrow stretch almost didn't accommodate the wide, stake-sided dray with Dan Rogers at the reins, but the man managed to squeeze through with four scraped hubs to show for it.

Fargo dropped back to ride alongside Karla's gray Studebaker farm wagon just before the night ended. "This does in my ideas for the night," Karla commented.

"There'll be other nights," Fargo said.

"As I said, I can wait." She laughed softly.

"Good," he answered. "Anybody know anyone else in this bunch before forming the caravan?" he asked.

"I don't think so," Karla said. "I didn't, that's for sure."

"Who formed the train?" Fargo questioned.

"Doc Anderson," she said. "He said he was too old to go it on his own and too poor to hire help by himself."

Fargo nodded, satisfied that the doctor had been honest in that appraisal. "How come Stacy Smith is lead wagon," he asked.

"The doc didn't especially want it and we drew straws," Karla said.

"There might be some changing around," Fargo said as he rode forward. He took his place again ahead of the wagons and watched as day began to slide down the funnel of night, letting the land take shape, become timbered hills and shale cliffsides, brush and downslopes covered by ivy, blood lichen and grape fern, wind-twisted mountain ash, and thickets of staghorn sumac. He fell back, met Stacy's eyes as she glanced at him, and he saw her straining to keep the weariness from shattering the cool, contained pose she clung to with such determination. Tension and the dark had made the driving hard, but he kept the wagons rolling until the sun came fully over the horizon. Riding on, he spotted an area under a rock overhang and, above it, a trickling waterfall that sloshed its way down from the high rocks. He waved the wagons to a halt under the overhang and dismounted.

Bobby and both Johnson girls had slept the better part of the night. They had energy to use and he put them to unhitching, feeding, and watering the horses. They were ready to sleep with the others before the morning was half over, and Fargo clambered onto a ledge, slid against the edge of rock, and fell asleep quickly, the silent wagons just below his perch.

He woke when the afternoon began to cool, sat up in the sun, and peered down at the wagons below. They were still and silent, and he spotted Bobby and Ada Johnson playing in a corner of the area, using sticks to roll a hoop between trees. The soft sound of the trickling waterfall beckoned, and he rose and climbed up to where the water fell idly from a small ledge onto a rock-lined basin to escape in rivulets into crevices. He undressed, stood beneath the trickling falls, and enjoyed the coolness of the soft spray. He turned his magnificently muscled body to catch the water as it bounced down erratically from the rocks above, stretched, bent his torso, flexed muscles, and heard the faint sound from behind a cluster of thick mountain shrub, a loose pebble dislodged to roll slowly downward. He didn't seem to look in the direction of the sound as he turned his body under the water, his eyes half-closed, but he swept the top of the shrubs with a slow glance and his nostrils flared as he inhaled deeply. He turned his back and the smile edged his lips as he caught the faint but unmistakable odor of powder and perspiration, not unpleasant, a musky, sexy scent of its own. He let his thoughts play, send his loins little messages, and he felt himself respond. He stepped from beneath the trickling falls, leaned back against the flat rocks, and faced the shrubbery, let thoughts continue to push at his body, and felt his powerful organ throbbing, growing, responding, the body answering the mind. He kept the smile inside himself as, with the hearing of a mountain cat, he caught the swift intake of sharply drawn breath. He let the sun dry his body a few minutes longer, and then he stepped to his clothes and began to dress. He drew trousers on last, enclosing the still-seeking magnificence of his organ and slowly began to walk from the little waterfall.

He chuckled silently, wondered idly as he slowly strolled to the wagons. The others were mostly up and outside taking coffee, and he let his eyes move across the site, paused at Stacy's wagon. The sliding door hung open and the smile stole across his face. He took a tin cup of coffee Doc Anderson proffered, sat down by himself, and sipped the strong brew. He was almost finished when Stacy, wrapped in a dark-blue robe, strolled down to the wagons. She started past him, staring determinedly straight ahead.

"Hope you enjoyed it as much as I did," Fargo murmured just loud enough for her to hear. If he'd harbored a doubt, it vanished in the rush of color that flooded into her face and down along her long lovely neckline. She hurried her steps to the wagon, almost running, and pulled the sliding door closed behind her.

Fargo laughed quietly as he emptied the coffee grounds at the bottom of his cup and got to his feet. "You can eat cold bird as we roll," he said. "Hitch up."

"Give me a hand, Bobby," Doc Anderson said to the boy, and Bobby started off beside the older man as Darrell Rumford stepped from his wagon. The sneer hung on his face as his eyes found the big black-haired man.

"How long you goin' to keep this runnin' by night?" he asked loudly.

Fargo saw Doc Anderson halt to watch, Bobby beside him. "Until there's no reason to keep doing it," Fargo said mildly.

"There's no reason now," Rumford said. "Some bushwhackers after us? Let 'em come, I say."

"Not till we have to," Fargo said.

The younger man's laugh was mocking and harsh. "Fargo

isn't much for standing up to trouble," he said to all within earshot.

Fargo turned away. "Finish hitching up. We'll be pulling out right away," he said, and ignored the frown on Bobby's face. He saddled the pinto, adjusted the cinch strap, and swung onto the horse.

Harlan Billings had emerged from his wagon clothed in trousers and a white silk shirt that outlined the folds of fat around his middle. Nonetheless, he mounted the driver's seat of the Conestoga with surprising ease to sit next to Zeke, who held the reins.

Fargo cantered to the front as the caravan began to move, slowed, watched them go by, let his glance go upward to the sky. Two more hours of daylight, he guessed as he rode to the front of the caravan and led the way to a gentle passage downward, rode for almost an hour when he turned and pulled alongside Stacy. He gestured to the slow downward lay of the mountain path that stretched ahead.

"Stay on this, keep heading south. It'll be dark before I get back, but there'll be enough moon for you to pick your way," Fargo told her.

"Where are you going?" Stacy said, and couldn't hide the instant alarm in her voice.

"Check out something. Don't worry. I'll be back. I might even take another shower for you." He grinned, saw her lips tighten as she stared straight ahead. He fell back, waved at Bobby as the boy stuck his head out one of the drop windows of the wagon. He let the other wagons pass him and seemed to fall back to the rear of the train, but he turned the pinto and rode away, staying on the road they had just traveled. He retraced steps and watched the dusk begin to settle. He'd ridden for an hour and the night began to bring down its inky curtain when he reined

84

up, the sound of hooves reaching his ears. He turned the pinto in through a grove of serviceberry, halted, and peered out through the leaves as the riders came into view.

The little man, Maxey, rode lead, looking like a black-clad gnome on the big bay horse. The others followed, faces showing fatigue. They'd been riding hard all day, that was plain, and they'd not try to follow farther as the night descended. As if to echo his thoughts, he saw the little man rein up and head into a small grove, hop down from the saddle. He watched the men wearily begin to bed down. They'd be in the saddle again come dawn, he knew, but the wagons would have had another six hours' headway. One more day was the most he could expect before the pursuers closed the distance. They'd already cut away a few hours. One more day, but it might just be enough, Fargo reckoned as he moved the pinto silently from the serviceberry, swung wide, and started to retrace his steps. Swinging wide, he cut in when he was far enough from the camped pursuers, yet it was more than two hours when he caught up to the wagon train as it slowly threaded its way down from the mountains.

He saw the canvas at the rear of the Conestoga pulled back and Harlan Billings lounged inside, emperorlike in his blue silk dressing gown. Emmy drove the platform-spring grocery wagon, he saw as he rode past. Even her driving was silent and somehow subservient, reins held closely together, arms in at her sides, her face totally without animation. The wagon hit a rut, dipped, shook, and he heard Darrell Rumford's voice from inside. "Jesus!" the man snarled, and Fargo saw Emmy slow the horses a fraction. He rode on, past Doc Anderson and the others, brought the pinto alongside Stacy's wagon. He caught relief in her glance before she covered it with her usual contained coolness. "Told you I'd be back," he said. "You stop to rest any?"

"No," she said, saw the disapproval in his face. "I thought it best to keep going," she explained.

"My fault. I should've told you to rest some," Fargo answered. He raised his arm, wheeled the pinto, and the wagons rolled to a stop. "Fifteen-minute rest," he said, dismounted, and helped Karla down from her Studebaker farm wagon. He saw Darrell Rumford, bare-chested, swing from the wagon and grab Emmy by the arm.

"Watch the goddamn holes or I'll whip your ass," he rasped, pushed her away. Her eyes stayed downcast as she gave no reply.

"Stinkin' louse," Karla spit out at Darrell Rumford. He turned, his face tight.

"Watch your damn mouth," he growled.

"Louse," Karla threw at him again.

Rumford took a step toward her.

Fargo's voice interrupted, quiet, almost casual. "Save your feudin' till the trip's over," he said.

Darrell Rumford halted, pulled his mouth into a harsh grin. "Why not?" he said. "You ain't worth gettin' steamed about," he tossed at Karla, and returned to his wagon.

Fargo felt Karla's angry glare. "I'm beginning to feel like little Bobby. I wonder if you would stand up to him," she snapped.

"Keep wondering," Fargo answered. He started to move on and saw Emmy, still outside the wagon, watching him. He expected the embarrassment he saw in her eyes, the submissive helplessness. But once again he was surprised by the flash of something close to dark fury he saw. The flash was extinguished as quickly as it had flared, and he walked on, climbed onto the pinto. "Move out," he said, rode forward alongside Stacy as she began to roll her wagon forward.

"You're a strange man, Fargo," she said, and he heard the cool amusement in her voice. "I heard what Karla Corrigan just said to you."

"And?" he questioned.

She turned a faintly smug smile toward him. "She was wrong, of course," Stacy said.

Fargo felt his brows lift. "You sound sure of that," he commented.

"I am," she said.

"How come you're the only one that's sure?" he asked with honest curiosity.

"I'm an expert at holding back," she said. "As you told me. I can recognize it easily."

He felt the smile cross his face, the answer both true and a spear tossed back. "That figures," he said.

Her eyes narrowed, then turned quizzical as she inclined her head to study him for a moment. "But I must confess I can't decide why you're holding back," she said.

"I'm saving myself," he said.

"For what?" She frowned.

"For you." He laughed and sent the pinto cantering away before she could muster an answer. He rode on ahead through the dark, followed the outline the half-moon permitted the land. The path was widening, leveling, and he suddenly felt the change in the terrain through the pinto's hooves, hard clay beds, and he grunted in satisfaction.

The dawn finally rose, pink-tipped, spreading itself across the horizon, and the flat land lay in front of him and he nodded in satisfaction again. He halted, let the wagons catch up to him, moved forward again. The caravan rolled out of the last of the hills and the Ruby Mountains loomed high behind them in the new day. The land would stay flat, dry, hard, interspersed with pointed hillocks of sand-stone until they reached the edge of the Monitor Range, and that would take days. He drove the caravan another hour and finally had them form a tight circle as they halted on the hard, flat plateau.

Sleep came quickly to everyone, exhaustion and the heat of the day saw to that. Fargo laid his bedroll between the Johnsons' farm wagon and the Rogers' big stake-sided dray. He had just pulled his shirt off when he saw Karla halt beside him. "I'm sorry about snapping at you back there," she said. "I guess I'm overtired. Or just frustrated."

"We'll be on a more normal schedule from here on, I'd guess," he said. "Just get some sleep. No hard feelings."

She nodded, satisfied at his answers. He watched her go into her wagon, turned on his side, and slept, one hand resting on the big Colt. The sounds of prairie creatures filtered through his sleep and his subconscious mind catalogued their harmlessness: sagebrush voles, kangaroo rats, pocket gophers, distant antelope, and the softly padded steps of coyote.

It was past midday when he woke, the sharp sound of a slap and a half-cry snapping him alert. He sat up, his eyes circling the wagons, halting as he saw Emmy step from the door of the grocery wagon. She wore a full-length nightgown and her high little breasts were surprisingly impudent. He saw the side of her face reddened, a faint trickle of blood from the edge of her left brow. But in her reddened face was an expression almost of triumph, of bitter laughter. She half-turned, saw him watching her. Emmy dropped her eyes and pulled the submissive cloak around her at once. She turned and went back into the wagon.

Fargo lay back, let another hour go by, and then rose, dressed, and rapped on the sides of wagons. "Time to move out," he said. He washed with the water from one of the casks as the others gathered themselves, emerged from their respective wagons, the Johnsons making the coffee.

"We'll be riding easy now," Fargo told them. "I expect we'll have company by the end of the day, but we're where I wanted to be."

"Where's that?" Dan Rogers questioned.

"Out here on the flat land," Fargo answered. "The mountain country was all in their favor. They could set up an attack from most anywhere. Out here in the open we'll see them come. No surprises and only clear shooting for us."

"You expect they will attack?" Doc Anderson asked.

Fargo shrugged. "I've got to expect that. They didn't come after us just to see how we're doing," he said. He rose, finished his coffee. "We'll be changing the wagons around," he said. "The Conestoga will be lead wagon, the Johnsons' big dray last in line."

"Now, just a moment," Harlan Billings said, getting to his feet, quivering flesh beneath the blue dressing gown. "I'm not going to be the first target for anything that comes along."

"We're all targets. Being lead doesn't mean anything," Fargo said placatingly.

"It does to me," the man insisted. "Don't you agree, boys?" he asked, looking at the two sullen-faced nephews. They both nodded as one.

"You're lead wagon or you can go it on your own," Fargo said, his voice suddenly steel. Harlan Billings exchanged quick glances with Zeke and Zach. The two men offered him no encouragement and Fargo saw the man's hanging jowls seem to hang further.

89

"You give me no choice," Harlan Billings said, acceptance in his tone.

"May I ask why you're changing the wagons around?" Doc Anderson asked.

"I want the two heaviest and slowest wagons front and rear. If we have to make a run for it, I don't want the lighter wagons outrunning the others, opening themselves and everyone else to being picked off," Fargo said.

Doc Anderson nodded in understanding and Fargo's eyes swept the others, included Bobby in his steely glance. "One more thing you'd best remember," he said. "That's the last piece of explaining I'm doing for my orders."

He turned, swung onto the pinto, and rode on ahead, halting a hundred yards out to watch the wagons roll after him, the Conestoga in the lead. He kept a steady pace, frequently wheeling the pinto to halt while he scanned the distant horizon behind them. The day was slipping away when he spotted the thin column of dust, still far behind, almost on the horizon line. He waited, let the wagons roll on, his gaze fixed on the yellowish thin dust column. Clay dust, he grunted, and he watched it grow quickly, sent up by the pounding hooves as they followed the wagon tracks. He turned the pinto and rode on, caught up with the wagons and saw faces tight with new tension. Bobby voiced the question for the rest as Fargo rode alongside Stacy, the baker's wagon now third in line behind Doc Anderson's light baggage wagon.

"Is it them?" Bobby asked.

"I'd guess so," Fargo said. "No Nez Percé or Navaho, not with all that dust."

Fargo kept the wagons at the same steady pace, and the pursuers gained ground until they were close enough to be in sight, still tiny dot figures in the distance, but nonetheless in sight. Night closed down quickly as the pursuers came into sight and Fargo rolled the wagons for another hour, called a halt, and had the wagons form a tight circle. He dismounted, had some cold grouse with the others as they made supper.

"Sentries tonight," he said. "Short, two-hour shifts. Everybody takes turns and everybody gets some sleep that way."

"You mean the women, too?" Dan Rogers quizzed, disapproval in his tone.

"I said everybody," Fargo barked, and his words shut off the protest that had started to form on Harlan Billings' lips. He set up a rotation schedule that put two sentries on watch at all times, more than enough to watch the flat terrain. He set Dan Rogers and Kate Johnson on the first shift. "You see anybody sneaking up, fire one shot," he instructed. He took his bedroll and set it down behind the oversize rear wheels of the stake-sided dray and let sleep come quickly.

He woke when Mildred Rogers and Zeke took over sentry duty, watched them take up their posts, and returned to sleep. He was awake again two hours later as Doc Anderson and Karla Corrigan came on duty, and when the dawn finally pulled itself along the horizon, he was awake, stood beside Harlan Billings.

"An entirely uneventful night," the man remarked.

"Good," Fargo said gruffly as he peered across the flat land to espy the distant horses outlined in the new light. He watched with eyes narrowed in thought as the others came awake, emerged from their wagons. Karla brought him a tin of coffee and he sipped it slowly, his eyes still on the distant shapes.

"I'm getting awfully hungry," Karla said.

"Patience is a virtue," he answered.

"Crap," Karla sniffed.

Fargo saw Darrell Rumford step from his wagon, pick up a leather water bag, and pour half of it over himself in an improvised shower.

"Easy on the water," Fargo said. "It's a long, dry haul till we reach any more."

"My water, I'll do what I want with it," the man rasped.

"The water belongs to everybody on the train," Fargo said.

"Not my water," Darrell Rumford said, pulling his face into a half-snarl. "My water's mine and I'll show anyone who says different." The challenge was there again in the bragging insolence, the swaggered stance.

"I hope there'll be no need for that," Fargo said. "Let's move out." He turned to the pinto and saw Bobby frowning at him, his eyes mirroring disappointment and something close to disillusion. He turned from the boy's probing stare and pulled himself onto the Ovaro, rode forward as the big Conestoga began to roll, Zach at the reins, Zeke beside him. Neither man had changed the sullen expression of their faces during the entire trip, he observed as he rode on, slowed when he was some fifty yards ahead of the wagons. He made a face as his eyes scanned the ground. The land had grown drier, the wagons raising a cloud of dust behind them. Drier, harder, a bone-rattling washboard surface to it. His eyes went to the distant horizon in the rear and saw the tiny figures moving after the wagons, again keeping their distance, apparently content to simply follow.

Fargo turned from the pursuers and kept the train moving through the heat of the morning, stopping only once to rest, then going on again, passed a succession of dry lakes with their shallow basins of cracked earth, which made them look like so many giant spiderwebs. He halted to water the horses in the middle of the afternoon and watched as the riders in the distance also came to a halt.

Darrell Rumford called from the tailgate of his wagon. "Want to ride back there and put daylight through the lot of them? Hell, there's not that many," the man taunted.

"Seven," Fargo grunted.

"Hell, I can take half myself," Rumford said.

"We'll just keep going our way," Fargo said.

"Shit, you're really afraid of trouble, aren't you, big man?" Darrell Rumford said, his laugh a harsh sneer.

"Never look for it. There's always enough around to find you," Fargo said calmly, let his eyes flick over the others listening. "Let's move," he said, and rode forward. Again, he stayed some fifty yards ahead of the wagons and his lips drew back in distaste as he watched the land grow still drier, the surface become lined with thick, hard surface ridges coming one after the other in parallel lines. He grimaced inwardly as he watched the lighter wagons skittering and bouncing over the unyielding ridged ground. Doc Anderson's light baggage wagon labored over each ridged topline, Rumford's wagon and Stacy's baker's wagon doing almost as badly. The two Studebaker farm wagons were taking it better, but not by much, and he wondered whose undercarriage would shatter first.

Behind them, the riders still followed, staying distant but doggedly following, not unlike a hungry pack of curs tailing a chuck wagon. When dark came and he formed a circle of the wagons again, the followers halted also, he saw. A small fire warmed the leftover rabbit and coffee washed it down.

"Same as last night," Fargo told the others as he drained his coffee. "Sentries, two-hour shifts."

"Why are they following us?" Mildred Rogers cried out

with a sudden explosion of tension. "It's driving me mad. I'd rather they did something, land's sakes."

"Don't ask for that, Mildred," her husband answered.

"Why?" the woman questioned again, and Fargo saw the others waiting for an answer.

"Could be different reasons," he offered. "Nothing to be gained by guessing now. Getting scared won't help, either. We'll just keep on our way."

"Much more of this and I'll wipe them out myself," Darrell Rumford said, the bragging barb in his words unmistakable. "Get me some more coffee," he barked at Emmy, pushed the tin cup at her. She took it, started forward, stumbled, and the cup fell into the edge of the fire ashes. "Clumsy bitch," Rumford shouted, gave her a push that sent her sprawling on the ground. "You clean the goddamn cup," he shouted.

Fargo saw Sam Johnson rise, start toward Rumford, Kate Johnson with fear catching her eyes. "I've had all I can take of you," Sam Johnson said.

Darrell Rumford whirled, and the gun was in his hand. "No, you ain't. You can have a bullet from me," he snarled.

Sam Johnson's hand stopped, still inches from his holster. In his face, Fargo saw not fear but the simple realization of fact, that he faced death.

"Sam!" The strangled cry came from Kate Johnson.

"Put the gun away," Fargo said quietly.

Rumford swung the gun at him. "You saying you're ready to take me on?" he prodded, the twisted smile on his lips.

Fargo's chiseled face stayed unmoving, but he felt the control needed to keep it that way. "I'm saying you'll get plenty chance to use that before this ride's over," he answered.

Satisfied, Rumford gave a harsh snorting laugh and

holstered the gun with a flourish. He sent a hard glance Johnson's way. "You were lucky this time, mister. Don't push me again," he said, and disappeared into his wagon.

Emmy waited a moment, and Fargo met her quick, direct glance before she followed her husband into the wagon. Fargo's wry laugh stayed inside him. Darrell Rumford hadn't been fast. Sam Johnson was simply not a gunman, his reflexes slow, cumbersome.

"Turn in," Fargo said, and helped stamp out the fire. He put his bedroll behind the big dray and slept almost at once, waking as each pair of figures changed sentry shifts. He rose when Emmy took her turn, and clad only in trousers, he moved to stand beside her and peer across the moon-tinted plains. He saw her eyes turn to him, move across the muscled shoulders, the expanse of his powerful chest, drop to his waist, lower further, linger, return to stare out across the flat land.

"What are you holding in, Emmy?" he asked softly, staring across the land with her.

"Who says I'm holding in anything?" she asked.

"Your eyes, little flashes. You've let me see them," he told her. "You know it, Emmy."

He felt her turn to him and he glanced at her. She was smiling and he knew the surprise showed in his face. Emmy's pinched little face was completely new as she smiled, but in the smile he saw the strangely triumphant, bitter-laughter expression he'd caught the night before in her face.

"When I'm ready," she said softly, held the strange little smile a moment longer, and then turned away to stare out across the flat land and the submissive, mousy air set into her face at once.

He stepped back, left her at her task. He lay down and slept, a light sleep that let him be aware of each change in

95

guards. He was first up when the day came, and he had the caravan rolling while the new sun was still peering over the hillocks in the distance.

The day became a carbon copy of the previous ones, the followers again content to stay just within sight. Fargo slowed the pace as he heard the near-crack of the undercarriage on Stacy's wagon as it skittered over the hard ridges. A wind blew a line of dust along the distant horizon, sending the yellowish cloud skyward in a half-circle, and Fargo watched with his lips drawn thin. When night came, he halted the wagons, saw their followers settle down in the distance. Like the day, the night promised to be another carbon of the previous nights, but when the meal ended, he saw the glow spreading upward in the night sky to the rear of the wagons. He rose, stared out across the land, and saw the orange-red glow grow brighter, taller. Doc Anderson, Stacy, Sam Johnson, and Karla came near to stare across the land with him. Dan Rogers drifted up and peered out with the others.

"Looks as though they've decided on a real roast for themselves tonight," the man commented.

Fargo's frown dug into his brow as he peered at the tall red-orange light. "They don't need a big-ass fire like that to roast a rabbit," he murmured, giving voice to the thought circling inside him.

"What do you mean?" Doc Anderson asked.

"That's no campfire," Fargo said.

"What, then?" the doctor pressed.

"It's a signal fire," Fargo said.

"Signal fire for what?" Karla cut in.

Fargo shrugged. "Maybe I can get that answer," he said. "I'll do some visiting. Sentries as usual here." He turned to the women. "Anyone got something white, a kerchief, a petticoat?" he asked.

"I've a white bonnet," Kate Johnson said.

"That'll do," he said, and waited as Kate went to her wagon to return in moments with the white bonnet in hand. "I'll wave this when I come back so nobody shoots an alarm," Fargo said. He hung the bonnet over the saddle horn as he swung onto the Ovaro. He jumped the horse lightly over the hitch on the ground between the Conestoga and the Owensboro mountain wagon, sent the horse trotting into the night.

The flame was a beacon, he reckoned, certain that was exactly its intended use. It would be visible for ten miles in any direction across the flat, dust-ridden plateau, he guessed. He rode at a steady trot and the glow became a fire with leaping, twisting flames. Nearing the flames, he heard the crackle of dry desert brush and driftwood they had obviously been collecting through the day. He rode as close as he dared, able to see the seven figures at the perimeter of the firelight. Sliding from the saddle, he ground-hitched the pinto, dropping the reins on the hard soil, and walked closer, another dozen yards before dropping down. He crawled another dozen yards on his stomach, inching his way until the figures by the tall fire were within earshot as well as sight.

The little figure paced around the fire in his black outfit, his face tight with anger as the fire began to burn down. "Son of bitches," he muttered, and took a half-hop, a little skipping motion, and continued his circling. The other men sat silently.

Fargo, prone on the ground, was the first to pick up the vibration of hoofbeats on the hard, dry soil. He stayed motionless, listening. The riders approached from the north and he lifted his head, peered through the dark, his vision cut off by the glow of the flames, which had dwindled down considerably. The others had heard the sound now and some rose as Maxey halted his circling, frowned into the darkness. Fargo watched the horsemen appear, counted six as they rode to a halt.

"Goddammit, where the hell have you been?" he heard the little man almost scream.

"Tryin' to find you," one of the newcomers answered, a long, thin-faced man with a narrow, lantern jaw.

"Shit, you had six days," Maxey countered.

"And you've been moving. It's not like you gave us a definite spot, you know," the lantern-jawed man said.

"I told you definite enough. All you had to do was follow the goddamn tracks," Maxey said. "You'd still be out there someplace if I hadn't decided to build the goddamn fire." The other man made no reply. "Bed down," Maxey ordered. "We'll make plans come morning. Now we're ready to move on them."

Fargo waited, watched the others dismount and Maxey fold himself cross-legged on the ground, his little figure nonetheless imposing in its own strange way, much as a bantam rooster cows larger fowl. Fargo watched for a few minutes longer as the fire burned itself down, and he slowly began to push himself back, staying on his stomach until he was safely into the darkness of the night. He got to his feet and reached the Ovaro in his long, loping, ground-devouring stride. One question had been answered, he grunted as he swung onto the horse. They had made no move against the wagons because they'd waited for reinforcements. But that was the only question answered. The central question remained, Fargo mused as he rode back toward the wagons. What prompted the extraordinary interest in this wagon train of misfit vehicles? He let his mind review the strange set of facts. First, they had to have been trailing the wagons to be on hand when the sickness struck. Then they wanted to bring it to its knees by denying it the much-needed medicine. That had grown clear now. They'd never intended to ransom the medicine for itself, because when they failed to get their hands on it, they sat back to keep the train under surveillance. Then the dogged pursuit and now the arrival of reinforcements previously called for.

It all added up to far more attention and determination than the average band of bushwhackers would bring to the average wagon train. Why? he grunted again. Did they simply think the strange caravan had to carry more money than the usual wagon train? Were they right? Fargo wondered. Or just mistaken? He couldn't discount the possibility that the little black-clad Maxey was a fourteen-carat oddball, a crazy who refused to give up on something he'd started. He was strange enough for it. Yet the explanation refused to satisfy, and Fargo found himself thinking of the stories each member of the train had given him for their presence in the caravan. He pushed aside further speculation as he reached the wagons, the white bonnet in his hand as he waved it back and forth.

Sam Johnson and Dan Rogers were standing sentry as he rode up and squeezed between two of the wagons. Their eyes asked the questions. "They got themselves help," Fargo said. "I'd guess they'll move on us tomorrow."

The two men exchanged sober glances. "We can hold our own, even with their help. We'll have the wagons as cover and the women can shoot. Kate can shoot straight as most men," Sam Johnson said.

Fargo didn't disagree with the man's appraisal. It wasn't incorrect, but the little black-clad man would realize as much also, and that made him uneasy. Fargo moved on, unsaddled the pinto, and lay down beside the big dray to make the most of the few hours' sleep before day came.

When morning arrived, he found Sam Johnson and

Rogers had spread the word. The others were gathered together, their faces a mixture of uncertainty, fear, and determination. Only Darrell Rumford wore his usual braggart's sneer.

"No magic answers," Fargo told them gruffly. "Out here we'll have time to see them coming just as we'd see an Indian attack, and we'll fight back the same way." He swung his saddle onto the pinto. There was no need for more words. "Get ready to move out," he growled, and the others drifted to their wagons.

Bobby was first atop the driver's seat, Fargo saw, his face flushed with excitement, high contrast to Stacy's grave expression. Fargo let the wagons roll forward and hung back, swung in behind the last one, the Johnsons' big dray. He followed, hanging back, his eyes flicking to the distant figures every few minutes. He saw them start to follow, still staying well back, and he rode after the wagons in tight-lipped silence.

The sun had risen into midmorning when he saw the line of distant figures suddenly start to grow larger. He halted, watched the horsemen come closer. They were on a fast canter, he guessed, watched, saw the horses spurt forward as the riders changed to a full gallop.

Fargo spurred the pinto on, caught up to the wagons in seconds. "Circle," he shouted, and saw that Sam Johnson had already begun to pull out of line to form the tail end of the circle. Zeke, at the reins, swung the big Conestoga around and the others followed, had their circle completed as the attackers came into clear sight. Fargo's eyes picked out the little man, sitting gnomelike again astride the big bay, hunched over the horse's withers. Bobby and the Johnson girls had been ordered inside the baker's wagon, and Fargo glimpsed their round eyes peering over the top of the drop windows. He lay down on the ground between Karla's farm wagon and the Rogers' dray. Stacy lay nearby, her fine-lined lips pressing so hard against each other they were almost white. She held an old Hawkens Brothers plains rifle, her knuckles tight around the gun.

"Don't shoot till you've a clear shot," he murmured. "And relax. You won't hit the side of a barn that way."

She glanced at him, her eyes round, no disdain in them now, and he watched her long breasts lift as she drew in a deep breath, then another, let herself grow less stiff.

Fargo's eyes swept the wagons. Zeke and Zach were positioned well. Harlan Billings tried unsuccessfully to hide his bulk behind the tail of the Conestoga, a heavy Remington .44 in his hand. Darrell Rumford, for all his bragging, was hunched up and well hidden beside his wagon, Emmy nearby, a musket in her hands. The mousy, submissive air in her face was still there, but with it a quiet contained calm. Emmy was a creature of hidden things, he decided. His gaze went out to the flat land and the attackers, who rode in a fast circle around the wagons, staying at a safe distance. Suddenly a half-dozen came in a little closer, staying at a full gallop, and let fly with a volley of shots concentrated on three of the wagons, the two Studebaker farm wagons and Doc Anderson's rig. They fired off the volley and raced out of range at once. Fargo heard the shouts of dismay, looked across to see the water casks riddled with shot, their contents spilling onto the dry, dust-covered soil.

"Damn," Fargo swore, swung around as another volley of shots slammed into two more of the wagons from the other side. Once again the water kegs split open, riddled, the water pouring out too quickly to try to halt. He cursed as he fired back, halted as the circling riders stayed away. He whirled, fired at four who started to race in close, and the others took up the fire with him. The four riders peeled off and raced away, but Fargo cursed bitterly as he heard the concentrated volley of shots from the other side of the circle. He whirled in time to see the water kegs on the big dray and on Darrell Rumford's wagon erupt in a gushing torrent of cool liquid.

He turned back to the circling horsemen, saw them move farther away, come to a halt in a wide circle that surrounded the wagons from a distance. They dismounted, lay flat on the ground to become almost impossible targets. The silence came to lie like a blanket over the flat land, and Fargo backed from beneath the wagon, stood up. The others followed, their eyes on him. "I wondered if they were just going to come at us," he said bitterly. "Now I know."

"They figure we can't last long in this heat without water," Dan Rogers said.

"They're absolutely right on that," Doc Anderson answered, his tired face hanging. "I'd guess perhaps another twenty-four hours."

Fargo nodded agreement as the others looked to him. "We'll be damn dried out under this sun by the time the day ends. The night won't help much. We'll never make it through another day's baking," he said.

"What do we do?" Mildred Rogers asked.

"There's not a hell of a lot we can do." Fargo told the woman. "For now we wait, hope for some kind of break."

"What kind of break?" Harlan Billings asked, and Fargo shrugged, turned away. He'd no answer for the question.

"Sit down, stay quiet. The less you move around, the less thirsty you'll get," Fargo said as he lowered himself to sit against the rear wheel of the Conestoga.

"I've never done much praying," Sam Johnson said, "but this is sure a good time to start." Fargo watched the man kneel beside his wagon, Kate joining him, the two girls coming to flank their parents. Karla sat with her eyes closed against her Studebaker and he found Stacy resting against her wagon, eyes open, her face tight.

"What do they want so badly on this train?" Fargo asked.

"Whatever we have, I'd say," Doc Anderson answered. "The usual things bandits take from people—money, jewelry, anything of value."

"Why else would they be attacking us?" Stacy said.

"Don't know," Fargo said blandly. "Thought maybe one of you'd be able to tell me." His eyes moved across the others, took in the shrugs and blank stares.

"Can't think of anything more than Doc said," Dan Rogers said.

Fargo nodded, put his head back, and closed his eyes. The sun burned down on him with almost mocking glee, too willing to do the bidding of those who used its awesome power. He sat with the stillness of a turtle on a log, yet by the time the afternoon was half over he felt the parchedness in his throat, the dryness of his skin.

Mildred Rogers had shed her blouse, sat in her skirt and chemise, her flat breasts and thick waist almost indistinguishable in outline. Darrell Rumford was perspiring profusely, he saw, the man's inner tensions backfiring. Harlan Billings kept wiping his face with a red kerchief. Zeke and Zach knew how to conserve energy, Fargo saw, the two men sitting motionless. Doc Anderson appeared to sleep, his head buried in his arms. Karla remained calm, he saw, keeping her eyes closed. A faint line of perspiration covered Stacy's lovely upper lip, he noted. Bobby crawled across the ground to sit near him.

"How far are we from water, Fargo?" the boy asked.

"I figure the first water we'd reach will be at the foot of

103

the Monitor Range. That's about two days away," Fargo said.

Bobby frowned and lapsed into silence.

Fargo closed his eyes and the sun burned down for another hour when Darrell Rumford's snarl erupted to break the sepulchral silence. "Goddammit, I say let's make a break for it," the man shouted.

Fargo's eyes snapped open. "You wouldn't get the wagon rolling," he said.

"Hell I wouldn't," Rumford snapped back.

"Try," Fargo said calmly.

Rumford's eyes went to the row of flat shapes encircling the wagons, his mind racing, calculating. He turned to where Emmy sat, her eyes watching, her face expressionless. Rumford stood up, the gun in his hand. "You take the reins. I'll cover you," he ordered.

Fargo saw Emmy's eyes meet Darrell Rumford with a long, level stare. "No," she said, her voice hardly audible.

"What'd you say?" Rumford frowned in astonishment.

"No," she repeated softly. "I believe Fargo."

"Goddamn, you'll do what I say," Rumford shouted.

"Not this," Emmy said, her voice quietly implacable.

Fargo saw the fury surging in Rumford's face as he cast a quick glance around, saw the others watching him be defied. It was more than he could let happen, Fargo saw. Only something to hit hard would halt him from exploding. "Try it yourself, Rumford," Fargo said. "Or are you afraid?"

He saw the man whirl, direct his rage at the remark. "Me scared? You out of your goddamn head, Fargo?" Darrell Rumford shouted. "You want a bullet between your damn eyes?"

"You think you can make a break for it? Let's see you try it," Fargo said again.

He saw the man lick his lips nervously, but the challenge was beyond sidestepping now. Rumford spun, started to climb to the driver's seat of the grocery wagon. The two enclosed sides offered some protection and Fargo watched as Rumford reached the top, started to swing himself around the sides to take the seat. The volley of bullets slammed into the left side of the wagon, splintering the partition at the outside of the driver's seat, smashing in the isinglass window. Rumford half-fell, half-dropped from the other side of the wagon, landed hard on the ground, and Fargo saw the fright in his face, his forehead trickling red from a sharp sliver of wood.

"Sons of bitches," Rumford hissed, stayed where he was, and pressed a kerchief to the trickle of blood. He half-turned, sat down with his back against the wagon wheel, his breath still in sharp drafts. His eyes sought out Emmy. "I won't be forgetting this," he growled. Emmy ignored him, stared into space.

Fargo rose, peered out at the circle of flat shapes, and saw the dusk creeping across the land. Dark would be on them in less than half an hour, he guessed. He swallowed and his parched throat hurt. He felt someone at his side, turned to see Stacy there, her face dry, drawn, and still lovely.

"Maybe we should try dealing with them?" she offered.

"They won't deal. They don't have to," he said.

"Then you're saying there's no chance?"

"There's time yet," he answered. "Don't give up. I'm still saving myself for you."

"Good God, how can you think about that at a time like this?" she flared.

"Hell, honey, there's only two things to think about at a time like this," he said. "Gettin' out and gettin' in."

5

Fargo stood motionless in the night, a tall, straight figure at the edge of the Rogers' big dray, his eyes peering across the darkened plains. Stacy had strode back to her wagon as the dark slid across the land and the others had mostly bedded down by their rigs, bodies already dried out, throats raw, the thirst an enervating, debilitating companion. Fargo watched, waited, saw the three-quarter moon slowly lift itself across the sky, grow high enough to cast a faint pallor across the flat land. He uttered a wry sound between hardly moving lips. As he'd expected, the circle of figures had crawled closer, not too close but near enough to let them keep a better watch in the night. With the dawn, they'd move back again to remain almost impossible targets pressed against the dust-covered, parched soil.

Fargo stayed unmoving as he peered at the circling line of flattened shapes and suddenly his nostrils flared and he lifted his head. The dry, hot wind blew over him, a sudden gust, sent a tiny swirl of sand curling around his feet. He waited and it blew again through the circle of wagons, and he heard Doc Anderson cough, watched him rise from where he'd been sitting and head for his wagon.

"It wasn't bad enough. Now this choking dust," the man muttered between coughs, shooting Fargo a glance of despair.

Fargo's head lifted again as another hot, dust-filled gust blew, seemed to suddenly vanish, then came again. He swallowed, felt the dry dust that had seeped into his mouth, and spat. It was an effort, he realized. He turned and stepped inside the circle of the wagons, halted beside Karla where she still sat unmoving against the wagon wheel, eyes closed. He saw her pull her eyelids open as he sank to one knee beside her.

"You've been awful quiet," he commented.

There was sadness in the little smile that came to her lips. "Thinking," she said.

"About what?"

"About how things never work out," she answered.

"Giving up? I figured you for the kind that would hang in," Fargo remarked.

"Been doing that all my life, hanging in," Karla said, resignation hard in her voice. "Guess I'm too tired for any more of it." Her hand came up, touched his cheek. "Too bad about missing out on that next time," she said. "Maybe another place, another world."

His smile echoed the rue in her voice and he rose, walked on. He'd nothing better to offer, but his eyes were narrowed as he listened to the loose sand blow across the ground as another rush of hot, dry wind pushed itself along the surface of the land. He spotted the small figure beside the baker's wagon and Bobby came toward him. "I was thinking," the boy began, and Fargo waited. "If I took a big leather pouch, maybe I could reach those mountains you mentioned and bring back some water."

"There's no hiding place out there. They'd spot you

riding off. You wouldn't get a dozen yards away," Fargo said.

"What are we going to do?" Bobby asked.

Fargo's eyes were hard as he peered into the night. "Wait," he said. "Sometimes help comes in ways you don't expect."

Bobby nodded acceptance, happy to embrace the hope, and Fargo moved on to lower himself onto his bedroll, stretch out, and let the night tick itself toward dawn.

He slept fitfully, waking each time to the rawness in his throat. The night was more than half over when he sat up, his ears picking up the skittering sound, the sand being blown across the ground as though a giant, invisible broom were sweeping the hard soil. He lay back on his bedroll, his eyes narrowed in thought, listening, and he felt the hot gust of wind blow across his face. He dozed some but the stirrings inside him refused to be kept down any longer—stirrings less than conclusions but more than idle hope. No marks, prints, trails, a different kind of sign this time made of harbingers he'd ordinarily view with alarm. Even now the excitement that caught at him was a grim, contradictory emotion, hope turned in on itself, hope laced with fear.

He managed a little more sleep and watched the dawn come, rose, each swallow a painful effort. He stepped outside the circle of wagons and his eyes went to the horizon in the new day's light. The hot wind blew in gusts and his eyes narrowed, his jaw growing set. The gathering had already begun, he saw, took on strength even as he watched. He lifted his voice to a shout and ignored the pain in his throat. "Everybody out. On the double," he called, his eyes remaining on the horizon.

Doc Anderson and Dan Rogers were beside him first, following his gaze. "My God, what is it?" Rogers breathed.

Fargo's eyes stayed on the yellow-gray cloud that rose up from the distant ground, spiraling, spreading, growing even as he watched it, ballooning outward in all directions to become a whirling, spinning mass. "Sandstorm," Fargo murmured. "Still getting itself together."

"Out of nowhere?" he heard Stacy ask, and saw the others had emerged to gather behind him, stare in horror across the flat plain.

"Not out of nowhere. Out of the dry, clay sand and the downdrafts of overheated air," Fargo said. "The air cools enough at night to start to move, circulate, spin. It starts to suck up the sand and feeds on itself until suddenly it explodes into what you're seeing out there, a roaring sandstorm."

"It's moving this way," Mildred Rogers cried out.

Fargo nodded, watched the whirling mass grow darker, move toward them with astonishing speed. He saw the black-clad figure of the little man called Maxey as he ordered his men to their horses, all eyes turned to the onrolling towering cloud. Fargo watched as Maxey and the others wheeled the horses and began to ride away, each man casting nervous glances back at the ballooning cloud.

"They're running," Bobby cried out.

"They have to run," Fargo said.

"Damn, we better do the same," he heard Darrell Rumford swear.

"No. We stay," Fargo said.

"Stay?" a half-dozen voices echoed the word.

"They have to run. It'll push them back miles on miles. They'd like us to run with them, but this is our chance. We've the wagons as shelter. They won't be perfect, but we can do it," Fargo said. "When the storm passes over us, we move on. They'll still be going the other way, staying ahead of the storm. I figure we can make up a day, at least."

"And if we can't weather it?" Harlan Billings asked.

Fargo shrugged. "I'd rather have Mother Nature do me in than those thievin' bastards," he said.

He waited, watched as the others looked in fear at the onrushing cloud of swirling, spinning sand. The day suddenly turned gray as the great cloud rose up to blot out the last trace of the sun. They had perhaps ten minutes, he guessed.

"Start moving those wagons," he said, breaking the moment of frozen indecision. "Leave them in a circle and the storm will swoop down, pick them up like a red-tailed hawk scoops up a fieldmouse," he said. The others began to move, gathering speed quickly. "Line them up side by side, two rows, with the horses in between," he ordered, pitched in to help Stacy bring her wagon around, then gave a hand to Karla. He put the Ovaro in the center of the other horses sandwiched between the two rows of wagons. He felt the first onslaught of stinging particles on his face and the day had grown almost black, the great whirling cloud towering, obliterating earth and sky. A terrible hissing roar began to shake the air. Five minutes left, he thought, grimacing.

"Lariats," he called out. "Circle the wagons with them. Tie them together, all of them." He started with his own lariat, pulling it tight around the square of wagons with the horses in between. The stinging particles of hard, dry sand were like tiny needles when they finished, length after length of rope wrapping the wagons together. "Inside," he ordered, "Lay flat, cover your heads completely."

He waited, watched Stacy push Bobby into the wagon. The closed doors would be a real help, the same with Darrell Rumford's grocery wagon and Doc Anderson's light baggage wagon. He felt a hand on his arm. "Come inside with me, Fargo," Karla said, pulled on him. He paused a moment more, his eyes all but closed to the stinging sands, squinted at the towering cloud, a whirling wall about to descend. He had gambled and the odds suddenly looked all bad. He tore his eyes from the awesome sight and flung himself into the wagon after Karla, tied the tail opening in the canvas shut. Karla tossed him a pillowcase and he lay facedown on the floor of the wagon, wrapped the pillowcase around his head. He felt Karla's body come against his, her hand find his, and suddenly the wagon shook, shivered, and he felt it half-rise, tilt, then fall back level again.

The terrible hissing roar surrounded him and he heard the sound of canvas ripping. The tiny particles of driven sand were as little needles piercing his shirt, part of his trousers, and only his feet and ankles, protected by boots, felt no pain. He felt Karla wincing beside him, heard her muffled half-cry. He could hear the horses bellowing in terror but too tightly hemmed together to be able to break away and flee. The wagon half-lifted again and he knew the others were also rocking, teetering in unison, and he shouted into the near-suffocating pillowcase, a muffled plea for the ropes to hold the wagons bound together. The wagon shook, rose again, quivered, and fell back once more.

Fargo felt the sand inside his shirt, his trousers. He moved a foot and pushed away sand on the floor of the wagon. Time stood still. They were in the center of some whirling, all-encompassing maelstrom in which nothing else existed, not earth, not sky, not air, only stinging, piercing, wind-driven sand. The howling went on outside and the wagon continued to shake until he feared it would come apart. His parched throat drew in a few precious gulps of air but it was painful to swallow. He caught the low moaning sound that was Karla's voice, sobbing into the pillowcase around her head. The wagon quivered again and suddenly the stinging sand ceased. He heard the hissing roar change to a lower, undulant sound, begin to drift away. He lay still, listening, and the sound grew fainter, fell away, and there was the silence, utter, tomblike, suddenly broken by the whinny of a horse.

Fargo reached one arm up and felt the sand cascade from his sleeves. He pulled the pillowcase from around his head and was struck by a small shower of sand. He sat up, glanced at Karla's figure half-covered with sand. The canvas side of the wagon was ripped away and over everything, sand. He helped Karla to her feet, took the pillowcase from her head, and saw her stare at him, shock drawn in her face, her eye blinking, and she slowly took in the realization that she still lived.

Fargo swung down from the wagon, landed in a stack of sand, and took in the sight before him. The ropes had held, the horses still jammed between the two rows of wagons, but covered with sand. Fargo saw the canvas on the Johnsons' farm wagon torn away, the Conestoga with only bare ribs left and a single strand of canvas blowing forlornly.

He watched what seemed a small mountain of sand move, lift, and saw Harlan Billings emerge, the folds of his jowls filled with sand to make his face appear drawn with tiny white lines. Fargo's glance sought out the baker's wagon and saw Stacy emerge with Bobby. Her eyes found him and they wore fear and shock.

"It's over," he said, and she nodded slowly as the others began to stir, emerge, most looking ghostlike with the white sand lying over them from head to toe. He looked much the same, Fargo realized. Doc Anderson tumbled out of his wagon to lay gasping on the ground.

Fargo let him take in air for a few moments and then helped pull him to his feet. "Hitch up," Fargo said. "We're moving out."

"Now?" Dan Rogers croaked.

"I've sand in my ears, my hair. I'm covered with it," Stacy protested. "The wagons are half full of sand, the horses coated with it."

"Some of it will blow away as we move and you can take care of the rest later," Fargo said as he started to unwrap the lariats from around the wagons. With Sam Johnson, he brought the horses out and ignored further protests. He helped Doc Anderson hitch up and the others grumbled but fell into line. Karla halted beside him on her tattered wagon.

"I never thought we'd come out alive," she murmured.

"Had a few doubts myself," he admitted. He moved on and with each step he felt as though he were standing in a sandbox. He took the pinto, let the horse shake off enough sand so he no longer appeared to be made of clay, and swung into the saddle.

"Roll 'em," he shouted, and heard his voice crack with dryness. He glanced back across the land. The monstrous, whirling cloud was still clearly in sight, driving everything before it that could run. That would most certainly include Maxey and his men. They hadn't time enough nor speed enough to race to the far ends of the huge sandstorm. They'd have to keep retreating before it until it spent itself, and he guessed that could take well into the night, perhaps the morning.

But he set a hard pace, ignoring the parched exhaustion he saw in the others. He rode back along the line a few hours later, checking the wagons, saw Emmy driving, looking not unlike a chalk stick.

"We must stop," Doc Anderson called to him.

"Keep moving," Fargo shot back. "We can make the foothills of the Monitor Range by night if we keep going. We can't spend another night without water."

The man's drawn, exhausted face peered forward as the thin body tried to find a last ounce of strength in it. They were all at the danger point, Fargo saw, but there was no other way. Survival meant reaching the foothills of the range before dark. They had to be revived and ready when the little gnomelike man returned to finish what Mother Nature had interrupted. And he'd return, Fargo grunted as once again the question prodded at him. Why? What drew him after these wagons? Plain thievery didn't bring that kind of determination. Fargo probed the question and came up with nothing more than he had before, questions that only brought more questions. He concentrated on riding over the dry, hard ground, knew he was pushing himself to the brink also.

The afternoon began to slide away, the sun almost over the horizon when he saw the land rise in the distance, the gray-green peaks filling the sky. He glanced back at the wagons, saw the others had seen it too, and he sent the pinto forward with a renewed burst of energy. The day still held night away as the foothills of the Monitor Range began to take shape, trees and brush forming the demarcation line between the dry, flat land and the soft soil and greenery of the hills. As they drew closer, Fargo's eyes searched the foothills and spied the last of the sun catching a downhill stream just back of the first row of hillocks. He veered, led the wagons toward the spot, reined up as they rolled up onto an incline of peppergrasses, the soft earth feeling like a pillow under the pinto's ankles. A small branch stream trickled down between a pair of rocks, clear and bubbling. He was among the first to fall on his stomach and gulp the cold water from the stream. He pushed himself onto his elbows after a moment.

"Easy, don't take in too much," he cautioned. He forced himself to wait, then drank again, more slowly this time. When he finished, he rose, saw the others taking in deep breaths as they lay on the grass, letting the luxury of water flow through their bodies. "The main stream's just back of those hillocks," he said. "Ladies first, gents next, and then the horses."

He watched Karla be first to begin hurrying over the hillocks, the other women following. His glance caught Emmy twisting away from Darrell Rumford as he tried to halt her. "I'm remembering how you spoke to me back there," he called after her. She hurried on, not glancing back.

"Unhitch the horses," he ordered, and took the time to unsaddle the pinto as the women bathed, the sound of their splashing easily heard. They had just finished unhitching the horses when the women began to straggle back, wet, faces shining, and he saw Emmy's two tiny, high little mounds outlined against the wet shirt, surprisingly inviting.

He started for the hillocks, reached the stream a few paces ahead of the others, stripping off clothes as he neared it. He plunged into the cold water, doused himself completely a half-dozen times before the sand was out of his hair and ears. The night was slipping quickly over the land when he finished, put on only trousers and boots, and returned to where the women were beside the wagons. With Sam Johnson, he took the pinto and three other horses, led them to the stream and let them immerse themselves. Dan Rogers, Zeke, and Zach brought more horses and the dark was almost complete when the last of the steeds had been washed free of clay.

Fargo led the way back to the wagons. Mildred Rogers was using a bucket to bail sand from the dray and he saw Stacy sweeping the white clay dust out of the wagon with a broom. "You can clean up tomorrow. Right now we're going to make another circle out there on the flat land," he said.

He saw Sam Johnson's glance of astonishment. "Put ourselves into the same trap?" the man protested.

"The same but different," Fargo answered, saw the others frowning as they listened. "I figure they'll catch up to us sometime near morning," Fargo said. "They'll see the wagons and figure we didn't expect they'd come after us. They'll be real pleased, only not for long, because the wagons will be there but we won't be in them. We'll be up here waiting, ready to cut them to pieces."

He saw Dan Rogers change his frown to a grin and Sam Johnson nodded. "Yes, I see," he rumbled. "The same but different." He let a short, pleased grunt escape him. "Let's get those wagons in a circle," he said.

Fargo went down to the flat land with the others as the night settled in. As the wagons were placed, he took in the line of rocks and the row of spreading, red-barked manzanita bushes. Between the two there was plenty of cover, he saw with satisfaction. He placed the circle of wagons a little over a dozen yards out on the flat land.

"Rifles," Fargo said, taking the Sharps from his saddle case. "I want every shot to count." He led the others behind the row of rocks and the thick manzanita brush. "Pick your spots, stay there, and sleep some," he said, aware that the order to sleep was gratuitous as he saw Karla's eyes close before he had time to turn around. Sam and Kate Johnson were settled against each other, Bobby

116

and the Johnson girls hard asleep in seconds to one side. Fargo led the pinto back behind a maple tall enough to hide the horse. He returned to the others, settled down, and allowed himself the luxury of heavy sleep, aware there was no way the little man and his thieving cutthroats could arrive before the night was on its way to morning.

He slept, the big Sharps cradled in his arm, grateful for the cool softness of the wind that blew gently down from the mountain range behind him. He woke with the midnight moon lighting the wagons with a dim pallor. The land was quiet, motionless, and he let himself sleep again, this time with the cat's sleep he had long ago come to master. The moon was at the far end of the sky, starting to dip behind the horizon line, when his eyes snapped open. He lay still, half on his side, one ear almost to the ground, and the distant vibrations came to him, turned into a faint sound, steady, drumming, hoofbeats on the dry, hard clay soil.

He rose on one elbow, watched as the horsemen finally came into view, and a thin smile edged his lips as he saw them ride closer, halt, and dismount. They proceeded on foot, crouching as they moved in.

Fargo's smile grew thinner as he watched the men spread out, start to encircle the wagons. He saw the little gnomelike figure hopping back and forth, using hand signals to place his men where he wanted them. Fargo glanced at Zeke, who slept nearest him; he reached out and placed a hand over the man's mouth. Zeke's eyes came open, stared at Fargo, and the Trailsman pulled his hand back, nodded out beyond the brush. Zeke peered, saw the figures that had positioned themselves in a circle, some half-sitting up, almost casually this time around. Zeke nodded, proceeded to wake Zach beside him. Fargo woke the Johnsons, who in turn woke Doc Anderson, and with the first gray glimmer of day everyone was awake, rifles in hand. Fargo's whisper was just strong enough to carry along the line.

"Karla, Stacy, Billings, Doc, Emmy, you take the nearest ones," he said. "The rest of you take the ones on the far side with me." He raised the big Sharps, picked out a prone figure, and fired. The sound of the shot was all but drowned out by the explosion of rifle fire that followed, but he saw his target half-leap from the ground like a flathead suddenly hooked and then fell back to lay still. He swung the Sharps to pick off another figure trying to get to his feet. The heavy bullet sent the man arching backward with his chest split open. Fargo's eyes swept the scene. His sharpshooters were doing well, the ground already littered with prone bodies. He saw three or four men had gained their feet, raced for their horses a yard away. One was the black-clad, gnomelike little figure, and Fargo saw him leap onto the bay, become almost invisible in the saddle. But he didn't streak out across the flat land as did the others. He sent the horse racing parallel to the foothills, and Fargo saw him swerve to charge into the hills as day began to light the land.

"Finish off the rest," Fargo yelled as he rose, raced to the pinto, and vaulted onto the horse. He wheeled the powerful steed, leaped a line of rock, and streaked across a slope as he glimpsed the black-clad little figure on the bay racing up into the hills. Fargo gained precious seconds as the pinto was able to take a sharp incline without missing a step.

Maxey was ahead, wheeling the bay through a mountain terrain of rock and brush, his little figure too small and hunched up in the saddle to afford a clear target. Fargo saw the man cast a glance back to see the black-and-white horse gaining on him. Maxey reined abruptly, sent the bay through a rock passage, and Fargo was at it in seconds, racing through it. He emerged on a slope laced with mountain brush and tall formations of rock, and he reined up sharply as he saw the bay, the saddle empty. He dived from the Ovaro as the shot whistled over his head. Hitting the ground, he rolled behind a stone, peered upward to where the shot had come from, and caught a flash of the little figure hopping zig-zag along the rocks.

Fargo fired, missed, and swore at his haste. He ran forward, caught another glimpse of the little man twisting and whirling as he ran, presenting a will-o'-the-wisp target. Fargo pulled himself up over a low boulder and saw the little man peering down at him. He let himself fall backward as two shots sent stone chips into the air a fraction of an inch from his head. He hit the ground on his back, fired at the black-clad shape that leaped a small chasm between two rocks, and saw the shot miss. He pulled himself to his feet and leaped upward, using rock footing to propel himself forward. A stretch of small rubblelike stones broadened out and Fargo saw the little man hopping and twisting as he ran. The Trailsman halted, aimed, fired, but the little figure half-leaped, half-hopped to the side and again the shot missed. Maxey vaulted over a small rock and disappeared behind a slab of slate. Fargo swore softly. The man was a damn kangaroo rat.

He pulled back and reloaded, stayed motionless against a rounded boulder, his ears straining. It took a few moments, but he finally caught the scrape of a spur against rock. Maxey was making his way around the top of the rocks, trying to circle behind him. Fargo let himself half-rise, peer, frown, pull back. The little man would have seen him, he knew, and he crouched, unmoving, hardly breathing. Again, the scrape of sound, this time a boot heel, almost directly above him. Maxey intended to pour lead down on him. Fargo half-turned, swinging his feet off the ground as he did to be certain there'd not be the slightest sound. He lay on his back, the Colt raised, pointed almost directly upward, his finger resting against the trigger. The black hat came into view, springing forward to peer downward. Maxey saw his victim below, tried to pull back, but he had committed himself, his gun arm extended. He couldn't correct quickly enough as Fargo's gun roared, three shots blasted straight upward. Fargo saw the gnomelike little face disappear in an explosion of red, the black hat, now half red, sailing into the air. The little man did his last half-skip, half-hop, this time in the air as he toppled from the rock above. Fargo rolled to one side, heard the body smash down with a sickening thud.

He drew a deep sigh, rose, and stared down at what was left of the strange little man. Whatever his reasons for pursuing the wagon train with such single-mindedness had died with him. Fargo strode back down the rocky terrain, found the pinto, and rode the rest of the way back to the wagons.

Sam Johnson came to meet him. "Three got away, one wounded, I think," the man said. "They hightailed out across the plains. They won't be coming back."

"I'd guess not," Fargo said. "We can hitch up and move on now." He took in the strained faces before him. "We'll bed down early, get a proper night's rest. Tomorrow we can repair the water casks and fill up."

He leaned against a flat slab of stone until they had their wagons ready to roll, and when he rode on, he kept the train on the soft soil in the foothills, paused often to drink from the little streams that rolled down from the high water in the mountain range.

They had gone into the afternoon when he heard the sharp, cracking sound, knew it for what it was at once, an undercarriage giving way. He spun the horse in time to see Emmy topple from the seat of the platform-spring grocery wagon as it crashed half on its side. She landed on hands and knees, shaken, bruised, but little more. He had dismounted when Darrell Rumford pulled himself from the rear of the wagon, his forehead red with a new welt. The man's eyes found Emmy, his mouth twisted in his usual snarl. "Goddamn bitch. I told you to watch where you're drivin'," he shouted, started for her.

Fargo stepped in front of him. "Wasn't her fault. Your whole undercarriage gave out," he said. "It was only a question of time. You can't take a platform-spring wagon on this kind of trip."

"You saying it's my fault?" Rumford growled.

Fargo shrugged. "I'm saying you had the wrong wagon. Make whatever you want out of that," he said.

Darrell Rumford's hand went to his waist and found he wasn't wearing his gun belt. "You're lucky, big man," he hissed.

"Maybe," Fargo said mildly. "Your wagon is still finished. Take the Scullys' Owensboro. Get your things transferred."

He turned away, walked to the pinto to see Bobby's eyes on him, and he ignored the question he saw there. Bobby turned, walked away, and Fargo waited while Darrell Rumford and Emmy put their things into the big Owensboro. When they finished, he waved the wagons on, rode up to where Stacy was glaring at Bobby as she prepared to climb onto the wagon. "What a terrible thing to say. Go into the wagon and stay there," he heard Stacy order. He saw Bobby obey, pull the sliding door closed with an angry gesture.

"Still trying the same approach, I see," Fargo said as he swung beside Stacy. She snapped the reins and the horse moved forward.

"You don't know what he said," she told him.

"I'm listening," Fargo answered, rode beside her.

"He said it was time for you to shoot it out with Darrell Rumford," she said, threw sarcasm into her voice. "Your little talk with him didn't have all that much effect. He's got a stubborn, wild streak in him, I tell you."

"He still wants somebody to care about. I'm not measuring up the way he'd like. You tell him how you felt about my hanging back?" Fargo asked her.

Stacy turned her blue orbs on him, disdain quick to circle their depths. "He doesn't give a damn what I think," she said.

"And you're not about to find out if he does," Fargo returned. "It's easier for you to keep thinking that. No involvement with the boy's feelings. Everything at arm's length." She refused him an answer, set her face coldly. "It might be fun at that," Fargo remarked casually.

Stacy glanced back. "What might be fun?" she asked.

"Showing you how to get involved." He grinned and rode on. He kept a steady pace through the foothills, the passages a little hilly but nonetheless much easier on horses and wagons than the dry, hard soil of the flat land. He rode on ahead, scouted higher into the mountains. The Monitor Range ran parallel to the Big Smokeyville and the Shoshoni mountains. The Nez Percé and the Shoshoni ranged all along the three mountains and he saw old tracks of Indian ponies but nothing to cause alarm.

He returned to the wagons as dusk came, set up camp beside a low hill with a trickling stream. Karla was backing her wagon into a space when the left rear wheel suddenly rode over a rock and Fargo saw her lose balance, pitch from the wagon to the ground. He was beside her at the same time Sam Johnson reached her. She grimaced in pain as he lifted her to her feet. "My back," she winced, doubled over.

"I've something that'll have it good as new by morning," Kate Johnson said. "Comfrey and oil of wintergreen. I'll rub it on later. You lie down meanwhile."

Fargo helped Karla into her wagon and the pain was in her face as she lay down on three pillows. She managed a wry smile. "This takes care of plans I had for tonight," she said.

"There'll be plenty of time." He smiled and left her to Kate Johnson. He led the pinto up into the higher hills until he found a niche between two rocks that was covered with soft, springy white-tipped moss and allowed him to look down at the wagons below. He unsaddled the pinto, nibbled on some pemmican, and stretched out in only trousers. The wagons below grew still quickly and he lay awake, listening to the night sounds and watching the blue velvet sky. The hills were still, only the scurrying of some deer mice interrupting the silence. The footsteps were easy to catch as they came into earshot, and he rose, moved to the edge of the rocks to peer down at the figure shrouded in darkness below.

"Fargo," he heard the voice call, and he was more than surprised.

"Up here," he said, stepped back, and lay down on his bedroll. The thin figure came through the little passage, halted, and he met Emmy's eyes, caught a strange light in their depths. She wore the full-length nightgown that made the two tiny mounds seem smaller than they were, yet somehow impudent. "Decided to talk some?" he asked.

"Decided a lot of things. Talk is last in line," Emmy said. With one, swift motion she whisked the nightgown over her head and flung it aside. He took in the thin, small shape, legs bordering thinness yet not unattractive.

The little breasts were high and perfectly round, each dotted with a flat, little pink nipple, and looked even more impudent. Her stomach was hardly there and a tiny, dark triangle made her seem as though she were perhaps twelve. With wings at her shoulder blades, she could have been a picture of a fairy sprite he'd once seen, a strangely sexy fairy sprite.

Emmy fell to her knees beside him, her hands pressing into his chest. She virtually leaped upon him, half-straddling him as she tore at trouser buttons. "Give it to me, Fargo. Give it to me. No, oh, God, no, now," she half-shouted.

He felt her stripping his trousers down and she fell onto his organ, pressing it against the little breasts, then to her cheek, kissing, caressing, and her rear end was pumping up and down. "God, God, oh, oh, now, now, oh, God," he heard her gasp, and the words became only little garbled utterances. The fury of her wanting became its own fire and he felt himself responding at once.

"Jesus, oh, Jesus," Emmy cried out, and straddled him, pumped up and down as she tried to impale her open, flowing lips on him. But her haste was frantic, all but out of control, and he heard her sobbing as she missed, came down on him again, and only succeeded in pushing him up into the tiny, dark triangle.

"Slow, Emmy, slow," Fargo breathed, but she seemed caught in a kind of frenzy.

"No, no, please, now, now, oh, now," she sobbed, cried, demanded, pumped herself up and down over him, missing again. He took her by the sides, lifted, his big hands all but encircling her rib cage. He turned her over as though she were a doll, and she pushed and heaved upward, struggling in his grip. He moved forward, slipped his pulsating thickness into her, stayed unmoving, filling her completely. "Ah . . . ah . . . aaaaaaaaaaaah," Emmy breathed, the sound a low, moaning breath. She tried to pump, move, but he refused to let her, held her completely still as he stayed inside her. "Ah . . . oh, God . . . aaaaaaaah," the long moaning cry came again. Slowly, he took his hands from around her rib cage, lowered himself atop her while staying completely still inside her.

"Easy, now, Emmy," he murmured. "Easy." He felt her hands lift, touch his face. Her little mousy, submissive face had vanished, replaced by a thin, steel-wire wanting. He saw her nod.

"Yes, easy," she murmured. "Please, Fargo . . . please."

He moved slowly inside her; she half-screamed and her eyes grew light, her thin neck arching backward. He bent down, took one high, impudent little breast in his mouth. The little nipple stayed flat, but he felt her tremble, start to move under him. She started slowly and the slowness vanished almost as it had begun and she was lifting under him, pumping, heaving, flinging the very inner point of herself against his filling organ.

Emmy's hands flicked up and down along his back and she quivered, shook, a frantic motion that refused denial. He began to move with her, quick, sharp pushings, matching the frenzy that was inside her. He felt her thin legs clasp around his buttocks, pull him into her, move, slide up and down his legs. "Now, now, now," she half-screamed. "Oh, God, now, now." She was heaving furiously under him, slamming her thin pelvis against him, and her body was aquiver from head to toe.

"*Ie!*" the sound suddenly burst from her. She heaved and pumped, shook and flung herself at him. He'd ridden broncs that didn't buck much harder, he found himself thinking. The sound came again, "Ie! Ie! Iiiiiieeeeeeeeee," and she rose up, seemed to hang in midair, screaming the sound into the night. He felt her little portal throb against him, as though a current were running through her. She screamed the sound again and her arms encircled him, the impudent little breasts two firm mounds pressing into his chest. He held her, continued to feel her quivering, throbbing portal until he heard the deep groaning sound rise up from inside her and she dropped from him, lay on the bedroll, her thin little-girl body seemingly out of place.

He lay forward, stayed in her, and she uttered a murmur of pleasure. He let the quivering fade, finally, slowly slipped from her, and she gave a tiny gasp of dismay. Her eyes opened, stared at him as she smiled. Her little face remained pinched, small, but now there was only a very female satisfaction in it.

"Jesus, you always like this, Emmy?" Fargo asked.

"I don't know," she said. "I haven't done it since I married that rotten bastard two years ago." She sat up and he decided the impudently round little breasts were extremely attractive. The nipples still stayed flat, he noticed. She smiled at the question in his eyes. "Mr. Bigmouth Darrell Rumford has never been able to get it up," she snapped. "He's a fucking fraud and you can take that any way you like."

Fargo felt his brows raise and his eyes stayed on the thin little figure. "That could explain a few things," he said.

"It explains why he keeps beating me. He's got to show he's a big man, but he knows I'm laughing at him all the time," Emmy said, and Fargo heard the cold anger in her voice.

"Why'd you stay?" Fargo questioned.

She leaned forward, turned, fitted herself against his chest and arm. "Same reason I married him. He told me he had an uncle who was going to leave him all this money once he met up with him. We've been chasing that uncle all over the damn country for two years.'

"Is that why you're really here in the train?" Fargo asked.

"That's right," Emmy said. "Only I decided there is no uncle. Darrell's been handing me a crock for two years now and I've been dumb enough to go along with it."

"Why'd you suddenly decide different?" Fargo asked.

"He slipped up a few weeks ago. He gave me the name of a different town than the one we were supposed to be heading for. He tried to take it back, but suddenly I knew he was lying. It was there in his face. He'd been stringing me along all this time, using me as a damn servant, beating me."

"This was getting back at him?" Fargo asked.

A sly little smile crossed the small face. "Just a beginning," Emmy said. Her body twisted away from his, legs raised, held primly together, then suddenly dropped apart, and she took his hand, pressed it against her moistness, "Two years is a long time," Emmy murmured. "I need more practice." Her arms pulled him to her and he followed, felt the excitement in it spiral at once. He thought the second time would be less frenzied. He was wrong, and finally she lay beside him, the little satisfied smile playing across her face. It made her look like a little girl that had just raided the cookie jar. "I'd best be getting back. He was asleep when I left, but I don't want him waking," she said. She took up the nightgown, pulled it on with the same quick motion she'd used to take it off.

Fargo got to his feet with her and Emmy Rumford seemed even smaller, thinner, but there was no mousiness in her face now, no submissiveness. He'd the feeling it would never return.

"What happens now, Emmy?" he asked gently.

The little smile stayed. "We'll see," she said, turned, and hurried through the path between the rocks.

Fargo listened to her make her way down until she was out of hearing. He returned to his bedroll and stretched out, felt warm and satisfied. Little Emmy had been an entirely unexpected dividend, and he slept soon, her eager warmth still with him.

Fargo woke with the morning sun that crept its way through the pathway between the rocks. He found the trickle of a stream nearby and washed, dressed, and gathered the pinto to begin the leisurely walk down to the wagons. He was halfway down the hillside when he heard the shouting and recognized Darrell Rumford's voice. He turned his gaze to the wagons below, saw Emmy run from the big Owensboro wagon, still in the nightgown. "Goddamn rotten bitch," he heard Darrell Rumford shout and saw the man leaping from the wagon after her, his face twisted with rage. "Goddamn bitch!" Rumford screamed, tried to seize her, but Emmy eluded his lunge, backed away. Fargo saw the others gathering, emerging from their wagons. "I'll kill you," Rumford shouted, grabbed at her again, but once more Emmy twisted away. Fargo saw her back, cast a sweeping glance at the others looking on, and he heard her voice, heard the pure maliciousness in it.

"Look at him, everybody, look at him," Emmy shouted. "Look at the weasel. He's been fooling you. He's no man. He's a damn fake."

"Bitch," Rumford shouted, lunged again for her, and again she avoided him. Fargo saw her turn on him, hands on her hips.

"You can't satisfy a woman. You can't even do it. But I don't give a damn anymore. I found a man. Fargo," Emmy flung at him. "God, is he ever a man! Fargo, you hear me, Fargo!"

"Whore! Goddamn bitch. Stinkin' slut," Darrell Rumford screamed.

Emmy stayed out of his reach and her voice taunted, speared, "Fargo, oh, God, can he please a woman. It was Fargo, you miserable little nothin'," she threw at him. "Fargo."

Darrell Rumford's mouth twisted in a snarl, his lips quivering as he swept the wagons with eyes of rage. "Where is he? I'll kill the bastard. Where is he? He's as good as dead," the man shouted. "Nobody touches my woman."

"Especially you," Emmy taunted. "Besides, I went to him. I wanted a man and I went to him."

Rumford spun, one hand on the gun in the holster, his face contorted with fury. "Him first. Then I'll see to you. Where is he? Where's that bastard?" The man spun again, swept the wagons with a quick glance, lifted his voice. "Come on out, you goddamn coward. You come out here, goddamn you," he shouted.

Fargo's lips were a thin line as he stayed motionless, half behind a manzanita. Emmy had struck back. She had planned it well, struck with devious cleverness. She had set Darrell Rumford up to be killed, giving him no other way but to avenge his pride, his braggart's pride. She knew, with female intuitiveness, that it would be no contest. She knew it and counted on it, and Fargo swore through his teeth. She was using him to do the job for her. He was her instrument of revenge and he swore at her damn cleverness.

He moved backward, turned the pinto into a clump of staghorn sumac. He glanced down at the wagons. Darrell Rumford was still shouting, calling for the man he wanted to gun down, and the others were shrinking back from his fury. Fargo saw Bobby to one side. The boy was the only one not looking at Darrell Rumford. His face was turned to the hills and Fargo wondered if he'd seen the Ovaro moving into the sumac. He turned away, followed the horse into the trees, went in deeper. He could hear Darrell Rumford still screaming.

"Come on out, you goddamn coward. You can't hide forever. I'm going to kill you, goddamn you," the man screamed.

Fargo saw a tall side of gray shale amid the trees, took the horse behind it, and was unable to hear the man's screaming any longer. He leaned back against the rock and felt the irritation pushing at him. Emmy had been more clever and more ruthless than he'd imagined, and he rebelled at how she'd made him a key part of her plans. Perhaps he could simply give Darrell Rumford time to cool down, Fargo pondered. The man was a bragging, hollow shell. He existed as a lie, bullying, deceiving, overriding others, but Darrell Rumford knew what he was better than anyone else. But Emmy had maneuvered him into a corner, a place where he had to play out his role. Yet perhaps time would restore his common sense, reason taking over for rage. He might even realize what Emmy had contrived to do.

Fargo's thoughts broke off as he heard the horse pounding up the hillside. He moved from the shale, peered through the sumac to see Darrell Rumford swing from the horse, his face still a mask of fury. "I know you're up here, Fargo. I knew you were a fucking coward. Come out like a man, you bastard," Rumford shouted.

Fargo drew a deep sigh. The man would come onto him sooner or later, He stepped out of the sumac into the open and Darrell Rumford spun to face him. Fargo's glance moved past him to the wagons below where he could see the others standing motionless, staring up to the hillside.

"You son of a bitch. You're a dead man," Rumford shouted.

"How'd you come up here looking?" Fargo asked.

"The kid told me. He saw you sneaking away," Rumford said. Fargo's half-smile was rueful. Bobby had simply done his own striking back. "I'm gonna kill you, you goddamn bastard," Rumford snarled.

Fargo felt his irritation spiraling again, not just at Emmy this time. Rumford was a cruel, sadistic, bullying woman-beater. The world would be little worse without him. He mightn't hesitate for a moment ordinarily, Fargo grunted, if only Emmy hadn't tricked him into being her errand boy. He still balked at that.

"Draw, goddamn you," Rumford said, cutting into his thoughts.

Fargo kept his voice calm, almost imploring. "Why don't you just go back down this hill and keep yourself alive?" he said.

"Draw, you lily-livered son of a bitch," Rumford rasped.

"You've been had, you dumb bastard," Fargo said, but there was only weariness in his tone.

"You gonna draw or do I blast you?" the man shouted.

Fargo didn't move, his arms hanging loosely at his sides.

Darrell Rumford's hand went for his gun. He had time only to hear the weary sigh that came through the big man's lips. His gun didn't come halfway out of the holster as the big .45 slug tore into his chest. Fargo heard the sound of the man's breastbone shattering and saw the instant deluge of red. Astonishment and horror flooded Darrell Rumford's eyes, hung there for a moment, and faded into blankness as he sank to his knees with a slow motion, swayed, and pitched forward onto his face. A circle of red seeped out from under his chest to stain the hillside.

Fargo turned away, his mouth a thin, hard line. He

slowly walked down the hillside, leading the pinto behind him, and the others watched in silence as he reached the wagons. He speared Emmy with a quick glance that she met calmly, without flinching, a hint of triumph in her eyes. "You want him buried?" Fargo asked coldly.

"I don't give a damn," Emmy said, and strode into the big Owensboro.

"It's only the proper thing to do," Fargo heard Doc Anderson say. "I've a shovel in my wagon."

"Be my guest. I don't give a damn either," Fargo said.

"I'll give you a hand, Doc," Sam Johnson said, and Fargo walked on. He saw Zeke and Zach watching him, their perpetually sullen faces unchanged, but their eyes held a new respect.

"Our mousy little Emmy has a lot of viper in her," Karla said as he passed, and he heard the tartness in her tone.

"Don't you all," he said, and moved on. He halted before Stacy, her round eyes watching him with what seemed a strange mixture of disapproval and grudging admiration. "Where's Bobby?" Fargo asked.

"Inside the wagon. I told him stay out of my sight," Stacy answered. "You know, he told Darrell Rumford where you were?"

"I know." Fargo nodded.

"I told you he has a wild, rotten streak in him," Stacy said.

"He did what we all do," Fargo said, and she frowned in question. "Something fails us, we try to destroy it, hit back at it."

"He still sent a man to his death and I told him so," Stacy answered.

"No, Emmy gets all the credit for that," Fargo said, and saw Stacy half-agree with a quick tightening of her lips. He moved on, waited till Doc Anderson and Sam returned from the hillside. When they were on their wagons, he motioned with his arm. "Roll," he called out, sent the pinto trotting forward. He estimated they had another four days of travel in the foothills of the Monitor Range with plenty of water and good soil underfoot. Why did he feel so damned uneasy? he wondered.

6

Fargo rode point most of the day, returning to check back on the wagons every few hours. Bobby had been uncommonly subdued, he noticed, sitting quietly during the rest breaks, not even responding to teasing by the Johnson girls. It was when they made camp and had just finished two fat ground squirrels Zeke had bagged, that Fargo saw Bobby moving toward him, his face grave. "You mad at me, Fargo?" Bobby asked.

"I'm not exactly happy with you," Fargo rumbled.

"I know," Bobby said, eyes downcast.

"Do you?" Fargo asked coldly.

Bobby nodded gravely. "I stopped thinking about the things we talked about," he said. "I won't stop thinking about them again, not ever."

"Better learn how to believe in people, too," Fargo said. "You can't do it halfway. That's no good. You believe all the way or not at all."

"What if you're wrong about them?" Bobby asked.

"You get hurt, sometimes a lot, sometimes a little. Comes with the territory, boy," Fargo said. Bobby let the words sink in as he slowly returned to the baker's wagon.

Fargo took his bedroll beyond where the wagons were encamped. He didn't expect visitors, didn't want any, and he slept quickly, soundly, and woke as the morning sun climbed into the sky. He dressed and returned to the wagons. Emmy checked the hitch on her horses and paused to turn stubborn, unyielding eyes on him.

"I did what I had to do," she said.

"You used me. I don't favor being used," Fargo growled.

Her eyes softened, a tiny smile came into the small face. "I'll make it up to you," she murmured.

"We'll see," was all he'd answer, and he moved on to saddle the pinto, found Bobby waiting for him.

"Can I ride with you this morning?" Bobby asked.

Fargo thought for a moment, decided he could send the boy back if he spotted trouble. "Get your horse," he said. Bobby was back before Fargo finished tightening the cinch strap under the pinto.

"I told Miss Stacy," he said, and swung alongside the Ovaro as Fargo led the wagons forward. He rode along the path for a half-hour and then turned upland, spurred the pinto higher into the mountains, Bobby tagging along behind. He halted once to peer down at the line of wagons as they moved slowly on below, and went on to a wide ridge. He rode slowly, his eyes everywhere—leaves, branches, grass, soil, brush—and he reined to a sudden halt and dismounted. He knelt down, his eyes on a set of hoofprints.

"Indians?" Bobby asked.

"No," Fargo said. "One rider, alone." He rose, looked back along the ridge, beyond where they'd picked it up. "Let's double back some," he said, and walked the pinto as he returned, moved beyond the spot where they had reached the ridge. He halted again, Bobby beside him, pointed to the set of hoofprints. "Yesterday's prints," Fargo said, gazed along the ridge again. "They go all the way back. He's been riding up here and watching us below." He turned, went back the way they had, continued on another hundred yards, watching the hoofprints continue along the ridge until he halted again and dropped to the ground. "He took off, here, went into a gallop," Fargo showed the boy. "See how the prints become deeper, dig into the ground at the front edge of the hoof?" Bobby nodded and Fargo climbed back on the pinto. "He rode along with us and then hurried on," he said.

"Maybe he was just riding along on his own," Bobby offered.

"Not likely," Fargo answered.

"Why not?"

"Man riding alone out here would be likely to ride down to visit with a wagon train," Fargo said. "This one didn't. He had to have a reason." He turned the pinto, waved at Bobby to follow, and rode down from the ridge to rejoin the wagons. He spotted a dozen Indian pony prints, but they were a week old and not worth being concerned over.

He called a rest when he met with the wagons and sat alone, his eyes peering up into the mountains. He looked away as Stacy came up. She managed to look composed and coolly lovely despite the searing sun, her yellow shirt clinging only lightly to the longish breasts. Maybe she was a damn iceberg, he frowned inwardly.

"Bobby told me about the tracks. You bothered?" she asked.

"I don't like things that go contrary to the way they ought to go," Fargo said. "Except for women," he added hastily.

"Of course," Stacy snapped. "I would have assumed that." Her eyes softened and she chose words for a moment, then proceeded. "I think everything that's happened, and the way you've handled Bobby, have gotten to him. I do appreciate your helping with him."

"Good." Fargo smiled broadly. "Now I can concentrate on helping you."

"I'd suggest you concentrate on getting us to California," she returned, and strode to her wagon.

Fargo waved the Conestoga forward, fell into line beside it. Harlan Billings reclined inside and Zeke and Zach spelled each other with the reins.

"I'm going to do some exploring. Any trouble, you fire three shots," he told the two men, and they nodded, their eyes following as he spurred the pinto up to the mountain land. He found the single rider's tracks along the ridge once more and followed the trail. The horseman left the ridge some half-mile on, threaded his way down a slope studded with alligator junipers, and Fargo followed to the bottom, continued on until he reined up to peer down at a square of print-covered soil. The lone rider had met up with friends, prints too scrambled to count, but he guessed at least a dozen horsemen. The riders had gone ahead, south, he saw, and he felt the soil. The marks all a day old, he grunted. He turned and made his way back, meeting the wagons and swinging in at the head of the train. Bobby rode up beside him and watched his eyes slowly sweep the trees and brush on the high ground. Fargo rode with a growing uneasiness inside him, that intuitive sense that reaches far past things seen, heard, or felt.

The day had begun to slide into dusk when Fargo felt his hands tighten on the reins. He had spotted the movement, and though he seemed to be staring straight ahead, his eyes were on the high land. He saw it again, the little motion in the line of junipers.

"We've got company," he murmured to Bobby.

"I don't see anybody," the boy said, casting his eyes back and forth.

"Watch the line of junipers up there," Fargo said. "See there, where the branches just moved?"

"How do you know it's not just wind?" Bobby asked in awe.

"Watch again," Fargo said. "Wind and a horse and rider move branches differently. They bend in the wind, a smooth motion. They don't quiver. They blow in the wind, they don't shake."

Bobby's eyes stayed round with awe as he fell silent. Fargo rode on a dozen feet ahead of the Conestoga. They'd gone not more than fifteen minutes more, he guessed, pulling up a fairly steep incline. They crested the top to find a stretch of level road and a half-dozen horsemen blocking the path. Another half-dozen looked down from both sides of higher land. Fargo let the entire caravan crest the incline before calling a halt. He was not more than a few yards from the six men across the path. He grunted silently. They might just as well have worn a name tag, all garbed in versions of their leader who sat at the center of the six. *Bandidos*, Fargo muttered silently, focused his eyes on the man in the center. Medium build, he wore a *poblano* atop a round face, a chin strap keeping the hat in place. Black, sharp eyes and a pencil-thin mustache that drooped at the corners gave his face a faintly evil cast. He wore two guns and carried two cartridge belts slung over his chest. He smiled and revealed a brilliant set of teeth.

"*Bienvenidos, muchachos,*" he said. "*Me llamo Carrillo.*"

"Fargo," the Trailsman said. "*¿Habla usted inglés?*"

"*Sí, amigo,* of course, Carrillo speaks many languages," the man said. He dismounted and Fargo saw the hint of a swagger in his walk. One hand stayed on the butt of the gun at his hip, Fargo took note. "We have been waiting for you, my friend."

"Waiting for us?" Fargo asked mildly. "I think there's some mistake." He felt himself thinking otherwise as he said the words.

The bandido leader stepped to one side, let his eyes travel back along the length of the wagon train and return to the big black-haired man in front of him. "No mistake Señor Fargo. This is the train that started at Jackpot in the north, the one with all the strange wagons," the man said.

"And you've been waiting for us," Fargo repeated, glanced back at Doc Anderson, who had moved closer. The physician shrugged helplessly.

"Sí, amigo." Carrillo smiled again and his teeth flashed.

"You come to show us a quick way to the California border?" Fargo said.

The man's smile was broad, a tolerant, chiding quality in it. "I like a man with a sense of humor, amigo," Carrillo said. "Carrillo is no guide. Carrillo is the greatest bandido this side of the border."

"Everybody's got to be proud about something," Fargo said.

He watched the man digest the reply for a moment and saw the little black eyes take on a glitter as Carrillo got the meaning behind the words. His smile took on an edge. "I hope, my friend, that our little exchanges will stay at words," the bandit leader said.

"That depends on you, amigo," Fargo answered. "Now, you say you've been waiting for us. Why?"

Again, Carrillo allowed him a chiding smile. "Please, Señor Fargo, don't waste my time with silly games," he said. His eyes took in the big man, whose face stayed calm, almost agreeable, but whose eyes were hard as blue gunmetal. "You are the wagonmaster, I take it," he said.

"Something like that," Fargo said.

"You have brought them this far. You must be either very lucky, very good, or very smart," Carrillo said.

"Maybe all three." Fargo smiled. "I also shoot real good," he added.

The man's brows lifted. "Words," he grunted in dismissal.

Fargo decided to seize the moment. Carrillo's kind respected one thing above all, force and skill. Fargo had glimpsed the diamondback sliding across a rock to the left of the bandit leader.

"Over there." He nodded and Carrillo turned around, his eyes widening.

"Carlos, get him. Aim carefully," Carrillo said to one of his men.

Fargo's Colt fired before the man touched his gun and the snake's head blew away. He dropped the gun back into the holster with casual ease and saw the bandit leader's eyes on him, still wide with surprise. The man nodded slowly at him. "You have made your point very, how you say, impressively," Carrillo said. His smile came again. "But the others do not shoot like you," he said.

Fargo cast an eye at the dusk coming in fast. He wanted to buy time and figured he could get at least overnight. "I want to make camp. We're all pretty damn tired. It'll be night soon. Why don't we continue out little talk in the morning?" he suggested.

The bandit leader shrugged and the tolerant smile came again. "What you really want is time to talk things over among you," he said. It was Fargo's turn to shrug concession. Carrillo clapped his hands in a gesture of decision. "I have no objections. Make camp where you wish. We will not bother you and in the morning perhaps we can settle matters with as little trouble as possible. You'll have your chance to decide overnight." He turned, swung up on a small, sturdy horse, and cantered away. The others fell in behind him and Fargo watched the riders on the high ground disappear.

"What was that all about?" Harlan Billings called from the rear of the Conestoga.

"We'll talk later. Roll them," Fargo said, moved forward with his jaw set hard. The bandidos seemed to have vanished, but Fargo knew they were watching from somewhere. He crossed the level stretch and found a place with a wall of rock at one side, good tree cover on the other.

Doc Anderson led the others around a small fire and his tired face seemed even more tired as he frowned at Fargo. "They're bandits, simply bandits," the doctor said. "You certainly can't believe they were really waiting for us."

"I'm believing," Fargo said gruffly.

"Why, in heaven's name?" Stacy cut in.

"They knew about the kind of wagons you're rolling and where you took off from," Fargo said.

"A good guess on that. And you said they've been watching us," Dan Rogers put in. "I think it's all just a clever approach, something to avoid a head-on fight. They're bandidos, these mountains are filled with them."

Fargo's glance swept the group. "I never understood why those other bushwackers were so determined to get at this train," Fargo said. "Now these varmints have been waiting. Somebody here has to have some idea why."

He waited as they exchanged glances with each other, vacant, mystified glances, he saw. Their eyes returned to him. "I can't answer that," Doc Anderson said. "There's no reason why this wagon train should be marked."

"Coincidence, all of it," Harlan Billings said. "Wagon trains are usually easy pickings, apparently."

Fargo's eyes came to Emmy and he saw her lips push

forward defensively. "Don't look at me," she snapped. "I only came on this goddamn trip because I was forced."

It was a partial truth, but Fargo didn't press.

Karla met his glance and shrugged. "I don't understand it, but I don't believe that greasy little porker, either," she said. "I really don't know why you do," she commented.

"I don't believe him. I believe the way the pieces are falling in place," he said. "Get some sleep. I'll see what more I can find out come morning." He rose, took his bedroll, and lay down some twenty-five yards from the wagons, beneath a manzanita that offered concealment and an open view of the campsite. He lay awake, thoughts revolving in his mind. Something was wrong. It had been wrong from the time he'd gotten into it. But were those on the wagon train as completely unaware of what it was as himself? They could be, he couldn't disregard that possibility. And Carrillo could have been given information simply not true. His lips drew back as he thought of Maxey. He would had to have been given the same untrue information. Again, impossible to rule out, yet dammed hard to buy.

Fargo stretched out. He'd play cat-and-mouse with the bandido come morning. It was a game Carrillo had long mastered, he knew, but the man plainly didn't want to rush in. There had to be a reason. Fargo closed his eyes, slept lightly, but the night passed without surprises. He rose early to find the others equally awake. "Everybody stays here till I get back," Fargo said.

"Tell them to go to hell. We took on the others. We can take these on," Dan Rogers said.

"Different breed. These are mountain rats, tougher, rottener," Fargo tossed back as he mounted the pinto and slowly rode the horse forward along the passage, which had narrowed considerably. He could feel eyes watching him and he kept a slow walk, halted as Carrillo and four of his men drifted out of the trees a few yards ahead.

"You have made a sensible decision, I hope, *amigo*," the bandit leader said and flashed his smile.

"No," Fargo said, and saw the glitter come into the black eyes. "I need answers."

"From me?" the man asked in surprise.

"I didn't set out with the wagons. I came in later," Fargo said. "What the hell do you think is on those wagons?"

The man peered at him, an appraising survey. "You are a very good actor, or you really don't know," he muttered. "You say you came to the train late?"

"That's right." Fargo needed.

Carrillo shrugged. "Maybe you don't know," He mused aloud.

"I've heard nothing but talk from you so far," Fargo said harshly.

Carrillo's eyes narrowed. "Somebody on that wagon train has a map showing where there is a store of ten thousand dollars in silver," the man growled.

Fargo refused to jump that quickly. "How the hell do you know that way down here?" he asked.

"That kind of information is hard to keep secret. One of my *amigos* was in Jackpot and heard about it. He told me when he came back here to the mountains," the bandit leader said. "The others who tried to stop you had heard it, too, of course. But as I never go north of the Shoshoni Range, I decided to wait and post lookouts. If you made it this far, it would be our good fortune." He smiled broadly. "Worth the gamble, and it has paid off."

"Not yet," Fargo snapped. "You ever think you got a bushel of shit for information? You don't know who or how? You ought to know that if you know so much."

143

The man's smile was chiding again. "I don't know who, but the information is correct. The map had been stained. Whoever had it had to have someone make a good copy," Carrillo said.

Fargo felt himself cursing under his breath. The man was too damned confident to be bluffing. He was turning answers in his head when he heard the hoofbeats behind him, spun to see Stacy racing up, fear and shock in her eyes. "They've got Bobby," she yelled. "Three of them raced in, took us all by surprise, and grabbed him. They were gone before we could turn around."

Fargo whirled to face Carrillo and his hand started for his holster. "Don't. There are six guns on you. You may kill me, but you will pay the price," the bandit said.

Fargo's hand twitched at the top of the Colt and he let it fall to his side.

"You bastard," he growled.

"A little insurance, *amigo*," the man said. "You will turn over the map of the silver or the boy will be shot in twenty-four hours, this time tomorrow morning."

"What if there is no goddamn map?" Fargo shouted.

"Mistakes happen," the man answered. "But there is a map." Carrillo turned his horse, pointed up to a level ledgelike area in the mountains. "The boy will be up there. You can see him shot if we do not have the map come morning," he said.

"My God," Fargo heard Stacy breathe as Carrillo and his men drifted away into the trees. His glance at her was sharp, studied the horror etched in her face, and he turned back to where the wagons waited, listened to Stacy, words falling over each other, tell the others of Carrillo's ultimatum. He watched the expression on each face, saw horror and shock on each, and he dismounted. Someone was a damn good actor or actress, he muttered silently.

He faced the group, swept them again with his eyes. "Ten thousand in silver. You could live comfortable the rest of your life on that," Fargo said. "It'd also buy a hell of a tombstone for Bobby Darrow." His eyes, blue steel, passed over the others again. "Somebody here is willing to do that," he said.

"That's unfair," Mildred Rogers protested. "Why do you believe that cutthroat?"

"It all fits, ties together. Carrillo is scum, but he happens to be telling it like it is on this," Fargo said.

"You've no cause to say that," Mildred returned. "You know why each of us joined the train. We told you."

"Most of you told me crap," Fargo barked. "I didn't press it then, but I am now. First you're going to give me the truth about why you're here. Then we'll talk about the map." He drew his gun. "Anybody lies will beat Bobby to a grave," he said.

"I told you the truth, Fargo," Doc Anderson said, his voice whining, and Fargo spun on the tired face.

"Try again," he barked. "You're too washed up to begin a practice with your brother. You're a man through with life, not one anxious to start fresh."

He saw the man's tongue lick his lips and Doc Anderson sank down on the sand. "It was a half-truth. I came to get to my brother before it's too late for me. I've had a bad ticker and I want to see him once more," the man said. "I made up the other story because I figured nobody'd go on a train run by a man with a bum heart."

Fargo grunted. "Probably not," he agreed, and his cold orbs fastened on Dan and Mildred Rogers. "You want to level with me while you can?" he rasped. "Dan here isn't retired. First, there are a hell of a lot of closer places to retire than wagon-training it through Shoshoni country to California. And the Amagosa isn't retirement country, anyway. It's too hard." Fargo saw the man and his wife exchange nervous glances, both wet their lips at the same instant.

"We're running," Mildred Rogers said. "From embezzlement charges. Dan worked for the bank in Marten's Hollow."

"I intended putting it all back. It just got away from me," the man said.

Fargo turned to Harlan Billings. The man's jowls shook as he grew instantly indignant. "You've no cause to doubt what I told you," the man said.

"You're an important businessman that has to get to California quick," Fargo said.

"Exactly, and what's wrong with that?" Harlan Billings frowned.

"Nothing, except that an important businessman who had to get the California fast would have taken the overland stage. There'd be five changeovers, but he'd be there weeks ahead of a wagon train," Fargo said. He took a step toward Harlan Billings, saw Zeke and Zach start for their guns. The big Colt leaped into his hands, fired, and the gun blew away from the holster on Zeke's hip. Zach dropped his hand.

"That's smarter," Fargo growled as he put the Colt into a fold between two of Harlan Billings' thick, hanging jowls. "Talk. I'm getting impatient," he rasped.

The man's jowls quivered and Fargo saw his thick lips move. The little eyes atop the mountain of flesh seemed almost to disappear. "I had some steady customers," he began. "For very young girls."

"You mean little girls," Fargo interrupted. Harlan Billings nodded, his jowls partly enveloping the barrel of the Colt. "I could do the world another favor right now," Fargo growled.

"No, please," the man said. "Zeke and Zach helped me. I directed the operation and they did the legwork. A lot of people up in Utah came after us finally and we had to run. Joining the train was as good a hiding place as any."

He drew the gun back, turned to Emmy. There was a defiance in her eyes. "Hell, you know all there is to know about why I'm here," she said.

"I know all you've told me," he corrected. "Maybe you got rid of Darrell for another reason! Ten thousand in silver all for yourself."

"No way," Emmy snapped, her small face hardened.

Fargo paused at Sam Johnson. "Never faulted your story, Sam," he said, and the man nodded. "Can't yours, either," he said to Karla. His eyes passed by Stacy.

"No questions for me?" she asked in some surprise.

"Not now," he said, and holstered the Colt.

"What does that mean?" Stacy snapped.

"Just what it said. Now we've got some truth about all of you. But somebody is still lying about that damn map," Fargo said.

"Not us," Mildred Rogers cried out shrilly.

Carrillo's voice calling from a distance broke in and Fargo turned, stepped to the far side of the campsite. "Here, Fargo . . . here is the boy. You can watch him for yourselves," the bandit leader said.

Fargo cursed silently. Bobby's small form was clearly visible at the very edge of the ledge of land. They'd tied his arms behind him to a stake driven into the ground. He felt Stacy beside him. "Those monsters," she hissed. "Those vicious, stinking animals."

"You're doing an injustice to animals," Fargo said as he drew her away. He went back to the wagons, sat down on a rock, drew Stacy down beside him. He had never seen her face so agitated, emotions no longer held back.

"We can't just leave Bobby up there to be killed," she said.

"He'll be killed faster if we try to rush them," Fargo said. "Carrillo would like that."

She buried her face in her hands and her eyes were red when she drew her hands away. She leaped to her feet suddenly, spit words at the others sitting in front of her. "What's the matter with you? You're just as monstrous as that cutthroat up there. You're willing to let a little boy die for your lousy pieces of silver," she accused.

"Don't look at me," Dan Rogers protested.

"You're all in it. Somebody is lying," Fargo said. "It'd take a week to search every damn wagon, so that's out. One of you has all day to look at yourself. One of you is carrying an innocent little boy's life in your hands. One of you is going to have to live with that for the rest of your life."

"I couldn't," Doc Anderson said, his voice weak. "I'm not the one."

"Nobody is," Fargo bit out harshly. "Only somebody's lying."

He took Stacy's elbow, drew her to the end of the campsite under a sumac. He lay down, stretched out. "We wait," he said. "Time and pressure will build up." His words held more hope than his thoughts. He lay back, let his mind go over each of those on the train again. He sought the little things, found a few but not enough, and the hours went too quickly. Stacy kept walking over to the side of the camp where she could look up at Bobby, return with her fists clenched. The afternoon was moving toward a close and no one had made a move. He grunted bitterly.

"No ideas?" he heard Stacy ask as she sat beside him, her eyes dark with pain.

He shook his head. "Could be most anyone," he said.

"Doc is a desperate man. That silver would let him live out his life in style. Harlan Billings has no goddamn principles. Sacrificing Bobby wouldn't mean a thing to him. Little Emmy is made of steel," He half-shrugged. "Too many candidates that could hang tough."

"What do we do about Bobby?" Stacy asked.

"We wait. It's all we can do now," Fargo said. He lay back again and closed his eyes. In a little while he heard Stacy get up to walk across the campsite and peer up at Bobby. He lay silently, thoughts turning fruitlessly in his head, and suddenly he heard the half-shout, half-curse leap from his lips. He sat up as the sound of racing hooves filled the site and he was just in time to see Stacy disappear on one of the horses. "*Goddamn!*" he swore as he raced to the pinto, vaulted onto the horse, and took off after her.

But she had cut up steep along the hillside and had too good a head start for the short distance. She was racing up toward a path that led to the little ledge. He went after her farther and heard the two shots crack into a tree branch over his head. He reined up, turned into the trees, waited. Barreling up the path was suicide, he knew, and he backed the pinto carefully from the trees, started to move down, away from the rifleman. He rode down to the level ground and turned to gaze up at the ledge. He hadn't long to wait as Carrillo appeared with one of his men and Stacy.

"Say, Señor Fargo, this *señorita*, she is very *encantadora*," Carrillo called, and seemed very pleased with himself. "She has come to stay in place of the boy," the bandit called. "Now, what do you think of that?"

Fargo's eyes shot hate at the figure on the ledge and swore at Stacy. She had finally decided to reach out, but she picked the wrong goddamn time and place. He knew

149

what Carrillo was about to say and the man did not disappoint him.

"I say now you have two fine hostages for you to think about till morning." The man smiled and Fargo saw two others appear with another stake, sink it into the ground beside Bobby, and tie Stacy to it. "It should help you, no?" Carrillo called as he turned away.

Fargo watched for a moment longer and then returned to the wagons. The others crowded at one side had heard and his glance was one of utter comtempt as he sat down beneath the sumac again. Stupid woman, he muttered to himself. When her heart went right, her head went wrong. But then, wasn't that usually the way it went? he reflected bitterly.

7

Fargo watched the last of the sun catch Stacy's dark-blond hair, send little shafts of light from it. His gaze went to the small figure tied beside her. He swore softly and his eyes moved across the others. No one moved, responded, offered anything except for Kate Johnson, who sobbed softly inside her wagon. He rose, peered up at the figures bound to the stakes, stayed peering up at them as the darkness closed them away. He walked to where Sam Johnson sat with his head bowed.

"I'm going to give it a try," he said.

Sam Johnson frowned back. "To rescue them?" Fargo nodded. "You're crazy," the man said. "You know they'll have both side passages leading to that ledge blocked. You'd run into a wall of hot lead."

"I won't be going that way," Fargo said. "I'm going up the face, right under the ledge."

"That's almost straight up, nothin' but a few rocks and vines and earth to hang on to," Sam said. "You could break your neck."

"Easy enough," Fargo said. "Worse, I could slip, make noise. They'd hear it and just blast me off there the way a horse flicks a fly off with his tail. But I have to try. There's no other way."

"Wait," Sam said, disappeared into his wagon. "Take this," he said when he reemerged. "A baling hook. You can get a good hold with this."

Fargo grinned as he took the slender steel rod with the big, curved hook at one end. "I sure as hell can," he said. "It could just make the difference. They'll be owing you, Sam." Fargo put the baling hook into his belt. "I'll send Bobby back down if I can. Keep him inside your wagon and get Zeke to stand gun with you. We can't give Carrillo any more trump cards." Sam Johnson nodded and Fargo turned to the others. Dan Rogers had started a small fire, for the mountain night wind was cool. Fargo's eyes traveled across the group. "One more time," he said.

He received only helpless shrugs, stares, and he turned away, the disgust welling up inside him. It was wrong to feel disgust for all of them. Only one was totally ruthless and uncaring. Yet for the most part, they had all turned into a fairly rotten, selfish lot. He turned away and took the pinto's reins, led the horse forward out of the camp, halted when he was almost directly under the high ledge. He left the pinto there. The moon hadn't come high yet and he wanted to make the most of that. He leaned back, gazed upward, the ledge impossible to see in the darkness. A piece of sumac near the bottom jutted out. Fargo pulled himself up on it, dug his foot into the soil, and began the climb.

It went easily at the start, enough vines and crevices to make for good climbing. But not more than a quarter up the steep, almost perpendicular side, the thick vines and rocky protuberances vanished, and he took out the bailing hook, drove it deep into the soil, felt it cut through the loose surface to catch hold in the firm soil beneath. He pulled himself forward, dug his heel into the side of the wall, held for a moment, brought the baling hook up farther, and hoisted himself forward. The action became the pattern for his climb, but he saw a line of creeping vines less than an arm's length away. He reached out, closed his hands around two, and swung himself over to them. He barely managed to get the baling hook up and into the soil as the vines gave way and his feet went out from under him. He clung, cursing silently, only the baling hook holding him. He got his heel into the wall, kicked a spot for himself, and rested until he restored balance and grip.

He frowned at the vines, reached up, took hold of another pair, and pulled on them. They seemed to hold and he applied more of his weight, The vines still held. He started to apply all his weight and saw them begin to pull away from the soil. They were strong enough to hold a seventy-pound boy but not a near-two-hundred-pound man. He made a mental note of the fact and began to pull himself upward again.

He'd gone halfway up the wall of soil when he halted, felt the muscles of his shoulders and forearms beginning to knot. Unable to stretch, flex muscles, he could only cling there and wait until the knots worked themselves out. Finally, he began the brutal climb again, grateful for Sam Johnson's baling hook. He raised the hook, drove it into the soil, and heard the clank as it struck a piece of rock. He froze, plastered to the side of the mountain, but the sound hadn't carried and he began to inch his way upward again.

The climb seemed hours and he had to stop and rest twice as his arms, shoulders, and leg muscles cried out in protest. But the second time he saw the ledge only a few yards above him. He also saw the moon beginning to swing across the sky. Soon it would bring more light than he wanted. He started to pull himself upward with new haste, dug the baling hook deep, and a stream of loose stones became dislodged, clattered down the mountainside, some hitting his head. Again, he winced and clung in place. He wondered if Bobby and Stacy had heard. More important, had anyone else heard? But there was no sound and he continued climbing. He was almost at the top and he glanced over to see that the strip of vines wound to the top of ledge. One more dig with the baling hook, his heel getting a hold in softer soil, and he pulled his head carefully over the edge of the ledge.

He saw, first, Bobby's round eyes staring at him, Stacy beside the boy. Fargo's gaze went past the two to scan the rest of the ledge and saw a half-dozen figures at the perimeter, all asleep. He was unable to pick out Carrillo and he pulled himself over the edge, lay flat for a moment at Bobby's feet. He took the slender, double-edged throwing knife from its calf holster and cut Bobby's bonds first, Two quick strokes, and the boy fell forward into his arms, clung there a moment. "You'll be all right," Fargo whispered into his ear, and Bobby nodded against him.

"Soon as the blood comes back into my arms," he whispered. He leaned back against the stake, started to rub his arms as Fargo severed Stacy's bonds. She slid onto her knees and rubbed her arms.

Bobby gestured to him. "I'm all right now," the boy whispered.

Fargo motioned to the line of vines. "You can lower yourself all the way down on them. They'll hold you," he said. "The Ovaro's at the bottom. Take him and get back to Sam Johnson."

Bobby nodded and Fargo watched as the boy began to lower himself off the edge of the ledge, grasp hold of the vines, and carefully test. They held and Bobby lowered himself another few inches, then another. The vines stayed solid under his weight and Bobby nodded, began to lower himself along the steep side on the thin vine ladder. Fargo felt Stacy beside him as he stayed crouched, watching Bobby go down until the boy disappeared out of sight in the dark.

"I won't make it down there," she whispered.

"Neither will I. That's why we're not going down," Fargo whispered.

She leaned her face into his cheek, her voice barely audible. "We can't get down the road out of here. He's got six men standing guard there," she said.

"Figured that," Fargo said, and half-rose, peered across the open space at the sleeping figures. They seemed all hard asleep, and he motioned to Stacy, started to move across the ledge in a crouch on steps soft as a cougar's tread. He moved slowly, carefully, watching the sleeping figures, and spotted Carrillo on the far side. Fargo's glance moved across the trees and shrubs that edged the back half-circle of the ledge, found an opening wide enough to move through without rustling leaves. But one of the bandidos slept only inches away from it and Fargo grimaced, yet made for the spot. The man, fully clothed, lay on his back, one arm tossed atop a thick serape rolled up alongside him. He was almost atop the man, motioned for Stacy to fall in behind him and follow in his footsteps. She started to obey when her toe stubbed a loose piece of stone. It rolled, just far enough to set up a small clatter.

Fargo saw the man's eyes come open. Shit, Fargo swore under his breath. There was no time for hesitating. They were dead if the other's woke. He saw the man's eyes blink, start to focus on him, and he moved to start to sit up. Fargo struck with the baling hook in his hand, bringing the huge hook down with every muscle in the blow. It plunged through the man's throat and out the back of his neck, embedded itself into the ground. He made a noise, but it sounded as though he were merely snoring, open-mouthed, short, guttural snorts. From across the other side, it would seem that it was indeed snoring. Fargo left the baling hook pinning him to the ground as it ended his life. He reached down, took the serape from alongside the man, and moved noiselessly into the woods, Stacy on his heels.

"I think I'm going to be sick," she gasped.

"You're going to be dead if you are," Fargo hissed back. He straightened, increased his pace, and moved upward higher into the mountains, glanced back occasionally to see her laboring to keep up with him. He paused at a place where the forest parted to let the moon light the two slopes and she sank to the ground, her breath harsh wheezing. His gaze picked up small bulges on the nearest slope and he lifted her to her feet, started forward. They were more than far enough from the bandits, but he wanted safety and he climbed for another fifteen minutes, slowed where the slope bulged out with brush covering a cave. He entered, listened, sniffed, and proceeded deeper. He turned and went back outside.

Stacy shook her head. "No, I'm not going in there," she said. "I hate caves." She shivered in the cool night wind and he shrugged. It would be dawn soon enough. He didn't expect Carrillo's men, but he'd easily hear them if they came. He spread the serape out and it turned out to be a huge one.

"More than big enough for the two of us. You'll get warm that way, too," he said cheerfully. Stacy shot him a glance laced with cynicism, and he shrugged, sat down on the blanket, doffed boots, shirt, and gun belt. He pulled his trousers down and rolled himself in the blanket, positioning the holster inches from his hand. He gazed up at Stacy as she stared down at him, her lips tight, and he saw the shiver course through her. "You'll freeze your little ass off standing out there for the rest of the night," he commented.

She tightened her mouth further, dropped to her knees, and he opened the serape for her. "I'm keeping clothes on my little ass," she said primly.

"Wouldn't have it any other way," Fargo said pleasantly. He wrapped the blanket around her, pulled her against him underneath its warmth, and felt her shivering finally lessen as he held her. Her hand rested on the smooth muscles of his chest.

"Won't they come look for us?" she asked.

"Doubt it. For one, they'll think we somehow got back to camp. Carrillo will be spittin' mad, but he's not the kind to let his anger make him forget the main prize. He'll keep his eye on the ball, which in this case is the wagons, where that map is waiting for him."

"How will we get back?" she asked.

"They'll quit that ledge by tomorrow, take up someplace else, and wait. He'll wonder what we're planning. We'll get back," Fargo said. He half-turned, brought her body around so that her left breast lightly rested against his chest. "Why'd you do it?" he asked not too gently.

She gazed thoughtfully at him. "I just did it. I thought maybe I'd shame somebody into coming forward," she said.

"Mistake," he grunted.

"Then I thought Carrillo would let me take Bobby's place," Stacy said.

"Little Miss Goldilocks," he grunted harshly.

"I guess I decided it had to be done. I couldn't let him just be killed," she said.

"You decided to get involved, stop holding everything at arm's length, only you picked the wrong time," Fargo said. "You get A for effort, though."

"I don't think I decided anything. It all just happened," she said.

"It's that way most times," he said, and his hand found her shoulder, slipped inside the top of her blouse.

"No," she said quickly.

"You started not holding back, reaching out, this is no time to stop," Fargo murmured. His hand moved down along the edge of her collarbone, felt skin smooth as the petals of a rose.

"No," she breathed, closed her hand around his wrist. He let his thumb extend, rub below the collarbone, to the soft beginning curve of one breast. "No," she said again, but she didn't pull his hand away.

He leaned over, found her lips with his, pressed them open. He let his tongue gently run along the edge of her teeth, across her upper lip. He moved the pink little messenger in deeper and Stacy gasped. Her hand stayed around his wrist, but she didn't pull on him. He dropped it lower, flicked the buttons of her blouse open. "Oh, no, no," she protested as his hand moved down the rose-petal soft skin, touched the long-curved breasts lightly, and he felt her body half-leap. She found a spurt of willpower, suddenly pushed against him, tore his hand from her.

"No, I won't," she bit out.

"Why not?" he asked, didn't wait for an answer. "You're sliding backward again." He pulled his hand from her, cupped one long breast with a firm grip, lifting it slightly.

"Oh, oh, God," she gasped. His lips moved down, found the pale-pink nipple. He didn't have to see it under the serape. It was well in his mind from that moment at the mountain pool. He blew upon the tiny tip and she quivered and half-groaned. His tongue came out, pressed down on the nipple, then circled it. Her arms moved, came around him, pulled back at once, and he felt the twitching of her torso. He pulled the breast into his mouth and she came hard against him, a half-scream torn from her, "Oh, oh . . . oh . . ." He undid her skirt, pushed it from her, pulled his underpants away, and lay his warm hardness against the inside of one willowy leg, and Stacy screamed again. "No, I can't . . . oh, please . . . I can't," she gasped as her hands pushed and pulled at him.

He put one hand over her lips, looked into her eyes, which held a mixture of desire and panic. "We might not get back," he said. "And if we do, you'll owe me again."

She stared back, emotions racing through her, and he moved slightly, brought the throbbing warmth higher up on her leg, and she drew her breath in sharply. His hand moved gently down along her navel, circled the little spot, traced a sensuous pathway down in a slow, circular motion, through the neatly dense little triangle, firm and springy, and he felt Stacy's legs come together tightly. He took a breast in his mouth again, played with it, caressed it with his tongue, the little virginal nipples with the edge of his teeth. She was moaning soft sounds now, but her thighs stayed clamped together, as much instinctive, protective, as in denial.

He let his hand drop below the little triangle, one finger explore, gently yet with steady pressure. He heard Stacy cry out as he touched the edge of soft lips. He pressed a fraction more and her thighs came partially open and he moved in at once to cup his hand around her softness. "My God, oh, no, oh, no . . . oh," she breathed. He parted the opening gently. She was just growing moist, the body overcoming the will. She was tight, perhaps virginal, he realized, and he slowed, let her catch up with her own spiraling desires as he stayed with his hand partially against the soft lips.

"Uuuuuuuuuh . . . uuuuuuh," she murmured, long, sliding sounds. He felt her hands press against his back, and she turned on her back, pulling him with her even as she kept shaking her head from side to side. He moved atop her, moved his throbbing, pulsating desire to enter, and she gave a little scream but her thighs rose, lifted, stayed waiting. He slid forward ever so slowly and felt her fingers dig into his back. "Easy . . . oh, God, easy . . . please . . . please, easy," Stacy was half-sobbing. He moved gently, felt her tightness around him, soft bonds of pleasure. He moved forward and back, and she screamed and now there was only wanting in the scream, protest and fear thrown away.

She began to move under him very slowly, a gasp of pain escaped her two or three times, and each time he halted only to have her pull on him, press against him. She had grown full wet and he moved in longer, smoother motions, faster thrustings. Her willowy legs fell open wide, then half-closed, fell open again as emotions seemed to overwhelm her ability to handle them. Suddenly he felt her half-rise, her hands on his shoulders, and she was trying to push him away even as her pelvis rose and fell with him. "No, no, no. I won't, I won't," she gasped out, her eyes closed.

He stayed still for an instant. "Why not?" he asked.

She lifted upward against him, pushed on his maleness. "Oh, God, I don't know why not," she cried out, and he thrust forward harshly, the first time he had done so. She screamed, yet demanded more. He pumped harder and she answered, but her hands had become little fists that beat against his shoulders and chest. "No, no, no, damn you," Stacy sobbed as he felt her tightening around him, felt the quivering pulse of her around his organ, and she arched her head back. "Ooooooooaaaaaaaaaaa," she groaned, a sound of rapture, defeat, a unique, special sound.

He moved inside her as she came with him and the sound exploded from her again. Finally, with a tremendous quiver that shook her entire body, she fell limply back on the serape. He stayed in her until he slowly pulled away. The first dawn light had come and he could look at the willowy loveliness of her, the longish breasts so beautifully curved at the bottoms.

He saw her staring at him, and her hand came up to run along his chest. "Why did I fight so at the very end?" she asked.

"I came across it only once before, but I've heard about it," Fargo said. "Some women have a real feeling of terror when that moment starts breaking. It's something to do with losing all control over themselves, I'm told. It's suddenly knowing you can't turn something off."

She lay back and was quiet with her own thoughts.

"Was it the first time for you?" he asked.

"Yes," she said. "There was another time, when I was a lot younger, a farm boy. I don't remember much about it except that I hated it and I don't think anything much happened."

"You hate this?" Fargo slid at her.

She gave him a sideways glance. "What if I said yes?" she asked.

"I'd say you were a damn liar." He grinned.

She sat up as a ray of new sun caught her dark-blond hair and strayed onto one breast. She gave him a half-pout. "You played on my conscience," she said. "All that about owing you for saving my life."

"Bull, honey. I tossed you that to give you an excuse to do something you wanted to do anyway." Fargo smiled.

She gave him a small glower and a coyness crept into her eyes. "Do we have to start back right away?" she asked.

"No," he said. "You've lots of time to tell me why you're really on this wagon train, Stacy, honey."

Her frown was instant indignation. "I told you that. The sheriff's office is paying me to bring Bobby to his relatives."

Fargo smiled pleasantly. "That story is as phony as the ones the others first handed me. I didn't call you on it the other day because I figured to get to it in time."

She continued to frown and managed to wrap herself in distance, though she sat beautifully naked beside him. "Why would you doubt it?" she asked.

"Because, honey, no sheriff's office has the money to ship a stray kid to California and pay a nursemaid for him, not here, not in all of Nevada, not anywhere in the whole damn West," Fargo answered pleasantly. He leaned toward her and his voice took on an edge. "Now I want the truth."

She pouted for a moment. "All right, the sheriff's office isn't paying for it," she said.

"Tell me something I don't know," he rumbled.

Her eyes flared for an instant. "It wasn't all a lie. Bobby was in trouble after his parents were killed in the fire. He was put into the sheriff's custody and I was called in to take charge of him. But only for a month or so. When Bobby's relatives finally answered, they hired me, sent me the money to bring him out to them. They also asked me to stay and look after him and they offered real good money."

"So why didn't you just tell Bobby the truth?"

"I was very strict with him," she conceded ruefully. "I knew he hated me. I was afraid he'd take off the first chance he got if he knew I was to stay on when we reached California. Telling him it was all on orders of the sheriff's office gave it an official status and let him think I'd be leaving as soon as we reached Thunder Rock." She drew a deep sigh. "I do want to stay on. They sound like nice people," she said.

Fargo thought aloud. "A day ago I'd have told you to forget it. Maybe now it might just work," he said. He glanced at the new day sky. "We can catch a few hours' sleep. I want to give Carrillo plenty of time to clear out."

She came against him, was asleep before he could draw his arm from under her. The morning sun had come high in the sky as he slept. He suddenly felt she was awake, her hand moving carefully, slowly down his body, exploring, probing. Her touch was light as a butterfly, delicate, trying not to wake him, yet eager to seek, delve. He lay with eyes closed, unmoving, as fingers trailed lightly down across his flat abdomen, over the thick luxurious brush, and ever so gently touched the resting rod of pleasure. He continued to remain absolutely still, but he felt himself starting to swell, thicken, reach out as her fingers moved lightly back and forth, and he heard her gasp, surprise first, then delight. He moved, opened his eyes to look at her, and she reddened in embarrassment. He took her hand, placed it over the now-throbbing organ.

"Oh, oh, oh . . . nice, nice," she breathed, and came against him, rubbing long legs up and down his body. "Again, please, again before we have to leave," she asked. "I want it again, please, please."

"Never refuse a lady," he said, and turned, let the pulsating tip rest against her lips, and she gave a little half-scream. She moved, pushed upward with her heels into the ground to push herself onto him. "Uuuuuuhhhhhh . . ." the long, moaned sound came from her again, a paean of satisfaction that reached back into the ages of woman. There was no protest this time when the moment came, only the tremendous wanting that consumed, devoured, obliterated all else.

She lay beside him, drawing in little breaths, her eyes closed and her fine-lined lips toying with a shadowed smile.

"Better than holding back, isn't it?" Fargo murmured as he kissed her breasts gently.

The smile became wide and her arms encircled his neck. "Yes, much better." She sighed, snuggled against him. He lay back with her, let her rest some, and finally stirred, got to his feet, and began to dress.

"Time to move, honey," he said, and watched her sit up, nod ruefully. He turned away from the pull of her willowed beauty and dressed hurriedly, had the Colt strapped on his hip as she finished pulling her blouse on. He led the way downward, taking pretty much the way they'd come in the night, and he finally glimpsed the flat ledge. He was a little off mark and he corrected his path, slowed, his eyes sweeping the area. Nothing moved and he reached the edge of the flat space, sank onto one knee, listened, peered along the brushline. "They've cleared out," he said, rising. "Let's make time."

He went down the pathway that led from the ledge, falling into his loping stride, glancing back to see Stacy making a valiant effort to keep up with him. He reached the bottom of the curving path, set out for where the wagons waited. "Damn, slow down," he heard her call, and he laughed, let himself rein in his long-legged stride. She came up beside him and he spied the wagons not far ahead. The others emerged as they reached the site and he saw Stacy's cool disdain take over. "I hate them all now," she said.

"That won't help," he said.

"Thank God you're back," Harlan Billings called out.

Fargo headed for Sam Johnson's wagon and saw Bobby race out, charge across the ground toward him. The boy wrapped his arms around the tall man's legs, clung there with all his strength, the gesture more than words could say. Finally Bobby pulled back and his eyes were shining as he looked up. "You know what Miss Stacy did, Fargo? She told that bandit she'd stay in my place, that's what she did. Wasn't that something, Fargo?"

"I'd say so," the Trailsman answered, and saw Stacy had paused, then started toward her wagon.

"He wouldn't do it, though," Bobby said. "But that's what she tried to do."

"She must care a lot about you," Fargo remarked.

Bobby nodded and cast his shining eyes around, saw Stacy heading toward the wagon. His little legs churned as he raced after her.

Fargo saw him take her hand as he caught up to her and he smiled quietly to himself. There's always some good in everything, he reflected. He turned, let his eyes move over the others, Emmy's thin high-busted form defiant in her very stance, Doc Anderson's tired face so drawn he seemed to have lost all blood. Karla's brown eyes met Fargo's gaze levelly as he moved on. Dan Rogers shifted uncomfortably, cleared his throat.

"Look, Fargo, I know what you're thinking, but the boy's back," he began.

"Not due to anybody here," Fargo said.

The man flushed. "I guess that's true enough. You did it, Fargo," Dan Rogers said. "But he's back. I say we just move on."

"Carrillo will have other ideas about that," Fargo said.

"He's got nothing to hold over us now."

"He's got enough," Fargo said, and his eyes were blue shale as he swept those in front of him. "Somebody here was going to let that little boy die," he growled.

"It does seem that might have happened," Doc Anderson put in. "But it didn't happen. It doesn't matter now."

"It does to me," Fargo flung back at them as he strode away. He went to the far side of the campsite, into the cool of the forest fern, and sat down against the grainy, scaly bark of a gambel oak, pushed his hat over his eyes. He closed his eyes, shut out the world. He had to think back, concentrate. He hadn't merely thrown an answer at Doc Anderson. It did matter to him, not just the terrible meaning of it, but that map might still be their one way out. Carrillo was not a man to give up when he was this close to ten thousand in silver. He let his thoughts drift back to the first moment he'd come to the wagon train. Slowly, he went over every single thing that had happened, tried to recall every little thing that had been said and done from that moment to now.

He was still deep in reconstructions, pulling memory into something more than memory, when he heard the footsteps approaching. He opened his eyes, pushed his hat back to see Sam Johnson. In surprise, he saw the gray-purple of dusk had slid over the mountains. "Didn't know the time had gone on so," he commented.

"Came to see what you're figurin' to do," Sam said. "You thinkin' about pulling out by dark?"

"Not tonight," Fargo said. "Carrillo will be watching us, but this is a good spot. He'd lose too many men coming at us here. I'd guess, come morning, he'll give us another offer. That might tell us something about what he's planning."

Sam Johnson nodded. "Good enough," he said. "I'll tell Kate we'll be staying."

Fargo leaned back again, closed his eyes. He wasn't finished searching for little things. The night came when he finally rose, stretched. He walked to where a small fire had been made and the last of a trio of black-tailed jackrabbits consumed. Stacy and Bobby weren't part of the group, he noted. "Sentries as usual tonight," he said. "Draw your own straws."

He turned, walked back to the baker's wagon. The sliding door was open and he saw Stacy and Bobby inside, Bobby asleep cradled in her arms. He paused by the door and Stacy smiled at him. "Lucky kid," Fargo said softly, laughing.

"You're next in line," she half-whispered.

"When the time comes," he said, stepped away from the door, and lowered himself to the ground in the darkness, his eyes sweeping those around the fire. He drew a deep sigh and waited till they began to retire to their wagons, the fire stamped out, Emmy, Harlan Billings and his mountainous bulk, Doc Anderson, Karla, Dan Rogers and Mildred, Sam Johnson, and the two perpetually sullen-faced aides to Billings. He watched them all go into their wagons and he waited, let the camp grow silent. He saw Zeke appear to stand sentry duty, let a few minutes more tick away. Finally, a terrible sadness filling the deep sigh that escaped him, he started toward the wagons, drew closer, turned toward one.

8

He knocked softly against the wood of the tailgate and stepped inside. Karla, drawing a robe around her, rose to face him, her brows lifting. The little smile toyed with her lips. "I didn't expect visitors, certainly not you," she said.

"Surprise," he grunted.

"You made a new woman out of Stacy Smith last night," she said, and there was tartness in her tone. "All I had to do was look at her when she came in. You must have done especially good work."

"I try," he said. "But this isn't a social visit, Karla."

Her brows lifted again. "Oh?"

"That map, it may be our one way out of here alive," he said.

Karla Corrigan's eyes remained quietly assured. "Why tell that to me?" she asked.

"Because you have it," he said.

"Are you fishing, Fargo?" she asked chidingly.

"You have the damn map, Karla," he said, and the growl moved into his voice. "Little things, they always do it. I kept going over and over everything that's happened and suddenly there it was, in front of me."

"You've been in the sun too long," she slid at him.

"When that little bastard had us pinned down without water, you were the only real calm one in the lot. The others kept wondering what they were after, why all this determination for a poor wagon train. I was one of them. But you, Karla, you were the only one who never questioned that. You never questioned it because you knew damn well why."

He saw Karla Corrigan's eyes grow smaller, a steel glint come into their depths. "And you were going to let that stinkin' bandido kill Bobby. You were going to sacrifice a little boy's life for that lousy silver." Karla's eyes grew still smaller and cold, merciless fury spewed from her face. "You are one all-time, prize-winning rotten bitch," Fargo said quietly.

"Get out of here," Karla hissed.

"Not till I get that map," he said.

"That map is the rest of my life with Tom," she said. "That map is all my tomorrows, and nobody gets his hands on it. Nobody, you hear me? Tom sent it to me because they were watching him too closely."

"Who was?"

"Pinkerton men. The silver's part of a stolen mine payroll. Tom worked at the mine. He was the inside man," Karla said.

"Stolen money and you'd let a little boy die for it," Fargo spit at her.

"The world is full of little kids who never make it. He would've been one more. That's the way it is. I told you, nobody's taking my tomorrows from me," she said.

"They were taken a long time ago. You just never noticed it," Fargo said. "You haven't got any tomorrows. All you've got is emptiness. There's nothing inside you. You're a mockery of a woman."

"Get out, damn you, get out," Karla shouted.

"I'm just surprised you were so good in the hay," Fargo said, and she picked up a hairbrush, flung it at him. He let it whisk past his head, turned to step from the wagon.

"Fargo . . ." he heard her call as he started out the tailgate, and he looked back. "You going to tell the others?" she asked.

"Afraid they'll come after you?" he asked.

"I just want to know. Are you?" she insisted.

"Not for now. You can still look them all in the eye come morning," he said, frowned as a fleeting expression in her face made him wonder if he'd hit a nerve. He walked from the wagon, his brow still furrowed. Karla Corrigan had turned out to be more than a surprise. She was a strange mixture, totally ruthless and uncaring, the kind who didn't give a damn what others thought. Yet she didn't want the others to know. He put aside trying to understand as he crossed the dark campsite. He'd just reached the pinto and his bedroll when he saw Stacy striding toward him, a light pink robe wrapped around her.

"I came out looking for you. A mistake, I see. A different woman every night, is that it?" she tossed out waspishly.

He spun on her, seized her by the elbow, and yanked her to him. "I'm in no mood for jealousy fits," he hissed. "Karla Corrigan is the one with the map."

Stacy's mouth fell open. "My God. How did you find out?"

"No matter. I put it together and I was right," he said.

"Did you get it from her?" Stacy questioned.

"She wasn't giving and it'd take too long to take her wagon and everything in it apart," he answered.

"Are you going to tell the others?" Stacy asked.

"No," Fargo said, his quick smile wry. "She asked that, too."

"No?" Stacy exploded. "Tell them! How dare you be kind to that monstrous woman? I don't understand you."

"I'm not being kind."

"Pity?" she snapped. "That's even worse. She doesn't deserve pity. She was willing to let Bobby be killed."

"No pity, either," Fargo said.

"What, then, dammit?" Stacy pressed.

"What do you think that fine band of upstanding citizens would do if they knew who had that map?" Fargo asked. "Harlan Billings, that child kidnapper, those two goons of his, Dan Rogers the embezzler, maybe Emmy ought to be included. She's proved she can be cold and deadly." Stacy stared at him, the very beginnings of comprehension setting into her eyes. "That's right, they'd go after it themselves," Fargo said. "They'd fight for it, all of them, like hound dogs over a bone, and Carrillo would wipe us all out."

Stacy's face had grown still, the truth of his words striking hard. "You're right, of course. I never stopped to think about it that way," she said.

"Right now the others don't really know that the map exists. I've got to keep it that way. They've got to stay pulling together to make it out of here. It's our only chance," Fargo told her.

"Yes, I know you're right. I just hate the idea of her even being part of the train now," Stacy said.

"You keep your temper in hand. Getting out of here alive is more important than Karla, now," he said.

"I'm sorry I bit at you so," she murmured.

"Been bit at before," he said as he spread his bedroll beside her wagon. He lay down on it and she was beside

171

him at once, wrapped herself tight against him, and he felt the anger inside her.

"She was going to let Bobby die," Stacy muttered. "She'd let us all die for her lousy silver. What kind of a woman is she?"

"The kind who's let life rob her of her soul," Fargo said softly. "Now get some sleep. You'll be needing all your strength tomorrow." Stacy pressed tighter against him and he heard her deep, even breathing in moments. He slept beside her, one hand on her back, the other on the big Colt beside him.

He woke her with the new day and she went into her wagon to dress. He used his canteen to wash and was dressed and ready to ride when the others started to emerge from their wagons. Karla was last and her eyes met his for a brief exchange—no fear, no remorse, no defiance in them, only a quiet containment. She had put on a white shirt and let her black hair hang loosely against it, and she looked as completely attractive as that night she had come to him. Was that her gesture of defiance? he wondered.

Stacy emerged, sent Bobby to play with the Johnson girls as Kate Johnson took morning-coffee chores.

"What do we do now?" Doc Anderson asked.

"Pull out," Fargo said. "I'll scout ahead. I want the children in Stacy's wagon, where they'll be closed in best." He had just drained his tin cup of coffee when he heard Sam Johnson's voice rumble softly.

"We've got company," the man said, and Fargo turned to look down the road. Carrillo and six of his men had suddenly materialized. He saw the bandit leader dismount, wait, hands on the two guns he wore.

"*Buenos días, amigos*," the man called. "It is time for our final talk."

Fargo strolled toward the man, showing his disdain by

172

letting his arms hang loosely at his sides. Carrillo noticed and returned a thin smile. "I took you too lightly, Señor Fargo," he said.

"I'll give you another chance," Fargo said.

"The map, *amigo*," Carrillo said.

"Nobody knows anything about a map here," Fargo said.

He saw the man's eyes harden. "Give us the map and you stay alive. If we have to take it, you will all die," Carrillo said.

"Anyone ever tell you you talk too much?" Fargo asked mildly.

The bandit leader's face darkened. "You are saying no to my most generous offer?" he asked.

"I'm saying go to hell," Fargo barked.

He saw the man's hands twitch at the top of his guns, but he decided better of it. "You have just signed your own death notices, my friend," Carrillo said, fury in his voice now.

"Maybe I just signed yours," Fargo returned. The man spun, pulled himself onto his horse, and sent the animal galloping away, his men following at once. Fargo returned to the others, met their fear-filled faces. "He'll pick the best place for himself," Fargo said. "All we can do is run and fight. First, everybody drives from inside. You can lay flat or sit, but you drive from inside. You drive from inside and shoot from inside. Got that much?"

"Yes," Dan Rogers said.

"We roll two abreast and stay that way. That adds protection and density. No matter what happens, keep two abreast," Fargo said. "I want the Conestoga and the Owensboro as the lead pair. Zeke will ride gun beside Emmy in the Owensboro. Stacy and Doc Anderson will take the number-two pair. Rogers, Sam Johnson, and Karla

Corrigan will bring up the end three abreast. I don't want any lone wagon tailing." He turned away and saddled the pinto as the wagons were brought into the order he had given. "Move out," he called, and watched as the wagons began to roll, no driver on any of the driver's seats. He grimaced inwardly. It was hardly much of a defense but it would have to do. He swung in beside Stacy and she saw him through one of the drop windows from inside, lowered the window to glare tight-lipped.

"That bitch. She could save us all," Stacy hissed.

"Once, maybe, not now," he said. "Don't open that window again till it's all over one way or the other." She nodded, closed the window, and he spurred the pinto forward. He moved on ahead of the wagons, lengthened the distance as his eyes scanned the roadway ahead and the land on both sides. There was more than enough cover for them to wait and race out from the sides. But they'd leave themselves wide open for return fire at almost-point-blank range. They'd suffer heavy casualties and fast. Carrillo was smarter than that, Fargo knew as he moved on along the road. His eyes swept the high land on both sides, most of it sloping too slowly to allow concentrated fire. He kept riding and had gone another half-mile when he reined up. The passage was suddenly bordered by two sides of rocky protrusions and he moved forward cautiously. It was the ideal spot, a place where they could pour fire down on the wagons, even though they'd not be able to see individual targets.

Fargo turned the pinto and rode back, met up with the train, and moved back and forth alongside the wagons. "When I say run for it, go all out and keep going until I tell you to stop," he called. "Understand?" He heard the murmur of voices from inside the wagons and turned back to ride lead.

174

It wasn't a long stretch. If they could race full out through it, they could escape with their skins. He slowed, saw the stretch of rock-sided passage loom up, waited, let the wagons roll closer. He wanted to let Carrillo grow confident. Abruptly, he turned in the saddle, yelled back. "Run, goddammit, run," he shouted, and sent the pinto into a gallop. He pressed himself low in the saddle, stayed hard along the edge of the passage. He heard the roaring rumble of the big Conestoga and the heavy Owensboro behind him, the others close behind. They were going full out and suddenly Fargo felt himself frowning. The sound of pounding hooves and heavy wheels was the only sound he heard, no gunfire from above, no fusillade of shots poured down.

He let the wagons move out of the passageway and waved them to a halt. "Walk your horses," he said, and swore silently. He had guessed wrong. Perhaps Carrillo had expected he would, the man applying his own pressures. They were succeeding, Fargo swore as he felt the dryness inside his mouth. He moved the pinto forward, his gaze continuing to sweep the high land and the low. The road began to curve sharply and he steered the pinto around the inside of the curve until it straightened. He stared ahead, felt his breath suck in, let the pinto go on another dozen yards before pulling the horse to a halt. He heard the oaths churning inside himself. Some fifty yards ahead the road grew narrow, became a bottleneck, and at the opening of the bottleneck, Carrillo and all his men were clustered, all with rifles aimed, ready to fire. Carrillo sat his horse, most of the others had dismounted, were jammed into the bottleneck, a few still on horseback behind the others.

It was more than a roadblock. It was a wall of firepower. It would be like running into a hailstorm of lead. "Shit!"

he heard Zach say, and he waited as the others halted in line, saw them stand up in their wagons for a better view.

"What the hell now?" Zeke muttered.

"The only thing we can do. Plow through them going full out. We've the weight and power. They'll have to break and run or be flattened," Fargo said.

"We'll never make it. They'll blast us apart with all that firepower," Zeke returned.

"Stay down, don't try to fire back. Just keep those wagons going full out and ram into them," Fargo said.

"It'll be suicide," Harlan Billings said. The others behind could hear the exchange, Fargo knew, and his answer was for all.

"We don't have a choice. We can't turn back. If they start blasting now, we'll be stationary targets, sitting ducks," he said. "Get down. Get ready to roll. Full out, every damn last ounce of speed you've got. Drive straight into them." He waited, saw the others behind begin to lower themselves out of sight. Harlan Billings made his mountainous bulk vanish on the floor of the Conestoga along with Zach.

Fargo started to turn to glance ahead at the bottleneck of rifles when he heard the thunder of hooves, the sound of a wagon gathering full speed. He spun around, saw Karla's wagon racing up from the last line, already at a full gallop, and then he saw a plume of smoke from the canvas. The smoke burst into flame, then another. He saw one side of the wood body suddenly erupt in fire as the wagon hurtled past him. She must have smeared axle grease over the entire wagon.

He wheeled the horse, half-started after her, but she was hurtling toward the roadblock and now the wagon was a rolling ball of fire. The front of the canvas burned away and he glimpsed Karla at the reins just behind the driver's seat, a blanket thrown over her. Pieces of flame licked at the blanket.

"*Shoot!* Shoot, damn you," he heard Carrillo scream at his men, who stared in astonishment and in horror at the onrushing wagon of fire. The bandits began to pour shots into the wagon, now but a few yards from them. "Stay in place. Don't move. Keep shooting," Carrillo screamed. But the furious volleys were passing harmlessly through the moving tower of flame.

Fargo saw the two rear wheels of the wagon afire, both rolling circles of red. He could only look on in horror with the others as Karla's wagon, a hurtling fireball now, trailing plumes of smoke, slammed head-on into Carrillo's men. He heard the screams of pain, human and equine, saw the wagon shatter, become hurtling shards of blazing wood. He saw one flaming wheel smash three of the bandits to the ground as though they were so many doll figures. One of the others not flattened or groaning on the ground tried to turn when a piece of burning axle pinned him as though he were a chicken on a spit.

"Move!" Fargo shouted at the others. "Get over there and finish them." He spurred the pinto forward, the bottleneck piled with smashed bodies, many aflame, pieces of still-burning wagon and slain horses. The hurtling fireball had all but wiped out Carrillo's entire force, and he saw the bandit leader race along the far side of the roadway, spur his horse up the slope. Fargo sent the pinto streaking after the fleeing figure, closed ground quickly as the Ovaro's powerful hindquarters took the slope without losing speed.

Carrillo turned in the saddle to see him, cut across the slope, slowed to get off three shots that were far off the mark. Fargo closed the gap further and saw fear join fury in the bandit leader's face. The man cut sharply, reined up for better aim. Fargo saw the surprise in his face when the pinto wasn't pulled up to evade the shots. Instead, flattening himself against the far side of the horse, half-hanging from the saddle, Fargo kept the pinto charging. Carrillo fired three more shots that whistled over the saddle, tried to turn to run farther, but Fargo was almost atop him. The Trailsman pulled himself back into the saddle and his shot grazed the bandit leader's temple.

Carrillo dived from his horse, hit the ground, rolled, drew his other gun, and came up firing. Again he overshot as Fargo kept the pinto racing forward, reined up, and leaped to the ground. Carrillo raced for the cover of a cluster of mountain brush. He was but one step away from it when Fargo's shot caught him, the big Colt .45 slug smashing through the right side of his rib cage to churn through his chest. The man staggered sideways, seemed suddenly drunk, staggered again, and sank to his knees. He looked up at the big man with the piercing lake-blue eyes with a last frown of awe and incomprehension. He fell on his side, rolled onto his back, and lay still. A slow trickle of red began to stain his two cartridge belts as Fargo walked back to the pinto.

Fargo sent the horse into a canter, hurried back down the slope. When he reached the roadway, only the odor of burning wood filled the air. The carnage at the bottleneck was a grim sight and Fargo saw the wagons halted nearby. Stacy came forward to meet him. "Karla's over there," she said, indicating a place where Doc Anderson, Sam Johnson, and Mildred Rogers knelt. The question was in his eyes and she answered it. "She's alive, but not for long. She's been badly burned, but she also took four bullets. She asked for you."

Fargo strode to the other figures and they moved back as he reached Karla Corrigan. They'd put a blanket over her that was already blood-soaked. He knelt down beside her and she felt his presence, opened her eyes. A wry smile somehow managed to touch her lips.

"It was too late for anything else," she half-whispered, pain in her voice. "It all went downhill . . . all of it."

"It did," he said.

"Fargo . . . I never wanted it like this, not any of it," she said. "You believe me?"

"I believe you," he said gently.

The tiny, wry smile stayed on her lips as her eyes closed and the final stillness came over her.

Fargo stood up, drew a deep sigh, and walked to the side, Stacy following, her eyes wide, full of groping. "Why, Fargo? Why did she do it?" Stacy asked.

"Conscience, second thoughts, and there was nothing left for her. Only the final gesture, to make up for what she'd almost done to Bobby," he said.

"For God's sake, why didn't she just give them the map?" Stacy frowned.

"Carrillo would have taken it and killed us anyway. I'd made a fool out of him, made him lose face in front of his cutthroats. She knew that. I knew it, too," Fargo answered.

"It all went downhill," Stacy echoed, murmuring the words. "That's what she meant."

"Yep." Fargo nodded. "The map wouldn't have bought any of us anything now. It was too late. It all went downhill."

Stacy's eyes were round, her hand light against his arm. "Did you believe her about the other, about not wanting it like this?"

"Yes," he said, "I believed her." He turned from Stacy, moved to Sam Johnson's wagon. "Get out all your shovels, Sam. We've a road to clear."

It was past noon when the caravan finally moved on. They'd put a simple cross on a wagon wheel for Karla's headstone off from the road and Fargo lingered a moment, let the others roll on. He finally turned the pinto down the road, aware once again that mistakes have a way of compounding themselves. Those of the flesh demanded a piece of you. Those of the spirit demanded all of you.

They had neared the end of the Monitor Range when night came. The California border, Thunder Rock, and the Amagosa Range were drawing closer.

Stacy came to his bedroll near her wagon after the camp slept, lay against him.

"I watched you and Bobby earlier. I think you're going to make it," Fargo said.

"I know it, thanks to you," Stacy said. "What about you and me, Fargo? Are we going to make it?"

He curled his hand around one long breast. "Every damn night from here to the California border," he said.

LOOKING FORWARD

**The following is the first chapter
from the next novel in the exciting new
Trailsman series from Signet:**

The Trailsman #21:
THE WHISKEY GUNS

*The Wyoming Territory in the early 1860s,
where the savage land began and
sometimes ended.*

The batwing doors of the saloon slapped open as the old-timer pushed his way into the hot midafternoon sunlight. Save for three saddle horses at the hitching rail outside Big John Golightly's Behind-the-Deuce and a black-and-white-spotted mutt snoozing in some heated shade on the boardwalk, Poe City's Main Street was deserted.

The old-timer spat through his whiskers into a dry wagon rut as his rheumy eyes, sunk in twin webs of crows' feet, picked up the dust cloud coming in on the Worland Road. He scratched himself, and suddenly the questioning expression on his hairy face turned to an appreciative grin as he caught the sounds coming from the open window just above him. A muffled scream was followed by whimpering, moaning, and some indistinguishable words. It was a woman's voice—entreating, urgent, finally demanding.

Chuckling, the old-timer scratched himself again and

started to amble across the street, half his attention on the approaching dust cloud, the other half on the pleasures going on in the upstairs room. A grin broke out all over him as the cries above mounted to the moment of supreme ecstasy.

In the upstairs bedroom at the Behind-the-Deuce Skye Fargo rolled off the girl, lay naked and content beside her on the big brass-postered bed. Both were drenched in sweat.

"Christ, Fargo. I heard you were the best."

"And now you know it," said the big, muscular man with the black hair and lake-blue eyes. He raised up on an elbow and grinned down at the blond-haired girl with the turned-up nose. His eyes dropped slowly down the length of the young, creamy body—the firm breasts with the still-erect nipples, the long waist and flat belly leading to the forest of black hair that spilled onto her still-quivering thighs.

"You never know in this world, do you?" he mused. "Here I took you for a blonde." His eyes took in her light-blond head of hair and his hand slid into the thick black thatch between her legs.

The girl's hazel eyes opened wide as her laughter tinkled across his face, "See, you got yourself two-in-one, a blond *and* a brunette."

"Which are you—really?"

"That's for me to know and you to find out, mister." And the tip of her pink tongue pointed out at him between her teeth.

"You're good-looking." And he added, "All over."

"So are you." Reaching over, she let her fingers run

lightly up his arm, stopping at the half-moon scar on his forearm. "What's that? A love bite?"

"Sure." He grinned. "Just a caress from a pretty mad grizzly."

She gazed up into his clear eyes while her hand moved slowly down his chest. "I'm glad you dropped in. My name's Ellen, in case you want to know."

"Pleased to meet you." Fargo grinned as he bent to her parted lips.

The girl's hand moved down his chest to the lean stomach, on down to his swiftly rising member. In a moment he had mounted her again.

Vaguely, Fargo heard the drumming of horses in the street outside, but he himself was riding Ellen vigorously, she responding in superb unison, her cries even louder than before as she urged him deeper into her bucking loins. Together they raced to the ultimate joy, their explosion simultaneous.

At that precise moment the bed gave way, the spring crashing to the floor, while at the same time from the barroom below came the roar of gunfire.

"My God, Fargo!" the girl gasped. "You arranged that!"

"Perfect timing," the Trailsman allowed ruefully as he withdrew from between her clutching legs.

The pounding on the door of the bedroom accompanied its bursting open.

"He's down in the bar!" The skinny little man in the baggy pants and bright-red galluses gasped the words, his eyes wild as he sprayed saliva into the room, staggering from the exertion of running up the stairs. "Son of a bitch brought a gang with him. Claim they're gonna tree the town, and by Jesus, that they be doin'!" More gunfire came crashing up from below and with it the sound of breaking glass.

"There goes Big John's mirror," the girl said calmly.

Fargo was already in his trousers, strapping on the big Walker Colt. "You sure it's him?"

"From your telling, it is him. Scar on his cheek, one finger missing. Mean-looking son of a bitch." Willie, the skinny lookout Fargo had left in the saloon below, was staring openmouthed at the naked girl, his eyes bugging out like the brass knobs on a set of harness hames.

Ellen merely threw the old man a look of distaste and without the slightest hurry sat up and reached for her clothes.

Fargo was already at the door. "Get across the other side of the balcony and cover me. See you again, Helen!"

"Ellen, for Christ sake!" But she was grinning happily.

"Hard to keep thoughts on business . . ." Willie grumbled as he reluctantly followed Fargo out of the room.

The balcony ran around three sides of the building, and now finding a good vantage point, Fargo crouched down to survey the scene in the barroom below.

A half-dozen men with drawn six-guns had the room covered, the big mirror in back of the bar was shattered, a lot of horn had been shot off the stuffed elk head on the far wall. Apparently no one had been hurt, the visitors having simply discharged their pistols in high spirits.

For a moment Fargo couldn't find the man he'd been tracking, but easing along the balcony now, he spotted his quarry. The lean man with the scar on his face was leaning with his back against the bar, a drink in one hand—the leader of the gang, apparently, for he hadn't bothered to draw his gun. Prine, Fargo didn't know whether he was

Maklin or Cresh; he only knew the name Prine. It had taken a long time and a lot of tracking. Yes. The long scar down the side of the pocked face, so well described by Pony Johnson back in Creede. Pony hadn't been clear whether Prine was actually one of the killers or was only an associate. In any case, he'd be a lead.

Fargo felt the old anger, but it seemed stronger now as it coursed through him. With a tremendous effort he forced himself to stay cool. Anger could ruin everything. He had learned the hard way not to let the excitement catch him, there had been so many false leads and disappointments, the countless searches that had proven fruitless. Still, he'd kept on—looking, asking, running down each rumor. He steeled himself now—with his quarry in his gun sight—to accept another failure if necessary. And at the same time he was more than ready for the kill.

He knew he could kill Prine easily right now. One shot would blow his head apart like a smashed melon. But it was not what he had planned. The confrontation was necessary. It had to be that Prine would see who was killing him . . . And why.

He had vowed that terrible bloody day that each of the swine who had killed his ma and pa and kid brother would be paid in full. It had been a long time since that day, the day that Skye Fargo had been born. He had already accounted for one of the three, the one known as Sledge. After Prine there'd be only one more. But Fargo knew how to be patient. He'd stopped counting how many false leads he'd chased. It might take him his whole life to get the killers, but he would find them . . . and he would kill them. He had vowed that years ago, taking the name Fargo, after Wells Fargo, the company his father had worked for—the name to remind him always and everywhere of his mission. Not that he really needed reminding; that scene was ever fresh in his mind, in his heart. Now, waiting on the balcony the big black-haired man's lakeblue eyes turned to blue ice.

Suddenly Prine was speaking, his little eyes on the group of customers who were beginning to fidget in their seats.

"We will have some funning, folks. Nothin' to get your asses in a uproar over, or about." And he chuckled, the sound coming out of his loose, wet mouth like a spluttering firecracker.

The crowd was silent; breathing could be heard in the moment following Prine's words. Behind the bar, Big John Golightly's reflection in the broken mirror looked grotesque as he ran the palm of his hand over his shiny bald head. He was sweating—a big man with very loose skin, pointed hands, and shoulders so narrow they seemed to disappear into his neck and head. His long body sloped toward his big hips, like a huge pear. When he moved his bald head now, the wattles beneath his chin quivered.

"Let the house buy you and your friends some refreshment, mister," he said, leaning stiffly toward Prine.

Prine kept his eyes fixed on the room in front of him, not turning his head even slightly to speak to the bartender at his back. "The house is buying a whole lot of things, friend. Including some of that fancy-pants stuff you got in them cribs upstairs. So get to loading them glasses for a start." And suddenly he snapped around like a whip to face Big John. "And I mean—right now!" Prine cracked out those words.

The room had not yet eased out of the tension, and now

the dark-faced, sneering man stepped away from the bar and barked. "Step up and drink, goddammit! I mean all of you. It's all on the house. And it is all in celebration of us boys come to visit. I mean all of you. I mean right now!"

He pointed to a man who had taken off his hat and was mopping his brow. "Step up here. You! Shit! Where is the faro dealer? We want to play faro. Where the hell is the son of a bitch?" He began banging his fist on the bar as his voice rose. "It says outside you got faro in this here place. Where the hell is your dealer?"

The men started to move toward the bar at Prine's invitation to drink, stopped in their steps now at the fury flying from him in every direction. Prine stood glaring into the silence in which everyone was frozen.

"He is right here," the calm voice came from the balcony stairs off to the gunman's right.

All eyes turned to the tall man with the black hair and lake-blue eyes who was coming slowly down the stairs, his big hands hanging loose at his sides. From beneath the wide brim of his hat the Trailsman's eyes seemed to grip the man standing at the bar, yet there was no expression at all on Fargo's face. Someone later remarked how he looked even more Indian than ever. Indeed, it was invariably at such moments as this that Fargo's quarter-Cherokee blood showed itself the most.

Prine sniffed suddenly and spat, not even aiming at the cuspidor near him. "You don't look like no faro dealer to me," he sneered.

"What's a faro dealer look like?" Fargo's words came out even as a milled board.

Prine's grin was a slice straight across his marbled face. And Fargo was thinking, Don't get mad, keep it easy, get him off balance, surprise the son of a bitch and get him off balance.

"Don't see no garters on them sleeves," Prine was saying. "Faro dealer ought to have garters on his sleeves. Don't see none on yours."

Fargo had reached the bottom of the stairs and had started to walk steadily toward the other man. "Figure you could give me a pair," he said, still advancing on Prine. "Like I could take them that you've got around your legs . . . you son of a bitch."

It was the sheer audacity of it. For a split moment the man standing at the bar was caught in stiff surprise, for all the time that Fargo had been talking he was walking straight toward Prine, as though he might crash right into him.

Fargo knew very well how to make use of surprise, shock, effrontery. As he said those last words, the smack of his open hand against the side of Prine's face was like a pistol shot. Almost within the echo of that slap, which spun the gunman half around, Fargo was behind him and had Prine's arm yanked right up between his shoulder blades, while his own other arm circled the gunman's neck, the wrist pressing relentlessly on Prine's Adam's apple.

"Don't move! I can break his neck and his arm at the same time!"

Half-drawn guns froze at those words.

"Drop your belts. Fast!" Fargo watched the hesitation.

"We can still get you, mister," a tall man standing at the side of the room said. "There's six of us."

The man in Fargo's grip gurgled inarticulately and tried to kick his feet.

Fargo's words were as clear as a fistful of aces. "Take a look up there on that balcony."

Heads turned to the shadowy outline of the gun that Willie was pointing down into the room.

"Willie's got a nervous finger on that cutdown Greener .12 gauge. That little scatter gun will cut you right off at the pockets if you even cough wrong."

Suddenly Fargo flung Prine away from him. The gunman fell to one knee, his face twisted with pain and rage, his arm bent and useless, as with his other hand he felt at his throat. Still nobody in the room moved. A sawed-off shotgun was nothing to mess with.

Swift as a whisper, Fargo had the big Colt in his hand. The guns clattered to the floor; he didn't have to say it again. He nodded toward Golightly, whose mouth was hanging open. "Collect the hardware, mister." His grim eyes swept the gunmen. "You'll get on and get out—right now."

In another moment the bartender had picked up the guns, and the six had started toward the swinging doors, Prine following.

They had just reached the saloon doors when the spotted dog that had been lying out on the boardwalk strolled in, passing easily beneath the flaps of the doors. Nobody paid any attention to the new arrival, save a large brindle cat coming from behind the bar who suddenly let out a screech and leaped directly at Fargo's legs as the dog started toward him. At that exact moment Prine spun around, his good hand streaking to a hideout in his shirt. Just for a split second Fargo's attention moved to one of the other members of the gang who had moved out of line.

Prine had the derringer out and up, but his shot was wild. Fargo dropped to the floor as a tall gunman hurled a chair at him. Rolling onto his back, he fired up at Prine. Two slugs tore into Prine's chest. Even before the gunman started to fall, Fargo was up on his feet with the room covered. The tall man who had thrown the chair had his arms stretched rigid toward the ceiling. Prine had spilled to the floor, his hand fumbling at the blood pumping out of his chest, his lips trying to mouth final curses, but no sound came.

"Too bad," Fargo said to John Golightly. "I was going to kill the son of a bitch outside, not to mess up your floor."

"Thoughtful," Big John said.

Fargo raised his head to the balcony. "You can toss down that broom handle now, Willie." And he watched the expressions on the faces of the gunmen who had turned back at the swinging doors to look as the wooden broom handle fell with a clatter onto the barroom floor.

"Holy shit!" Big John Golightly's eyes bugged right out of his head. "You have got balls, mister!"

"And I aim to keep 'em," Fargo said.

He was looking down at the body of Prine. He had felt it almost the moment he had pulled the trigger of the Colt. Something wrong. And as he watched the blood spreading all over Prine's hickory shirt, as he saw Prine going with hatred to his death, Fargo knew for sure. Looking at Prine's hand he saw quite clearly that he had not shot one of the men who had murdered his family. The gunman was indeed missing his little finger—but on the wrong hand.

Exciting Westerns by Jon Sharpe from SIGNET

(0451)

☐ **THE TRAILSMAN #1: SEVEN WAGONS WEST**

(127293—$2.50)*

☐ **THE TRAILSMAN #2: THE HANGING TRAIL** (110536—$2.25)

☐ **THE TRAILSMAN #3: MOUNTAIN MAN KILL** (121007—$2.50)*

☐ **THE TRAILSMAN #4: THE SUNDOWN SEARCHERS**

(122003—$2.50)*

☐ **THE TRAILSMAN #5: THE RIVER RAIDERS** (127188—$2.50)*

☐ **THE TRAILSMAN #6: DAKOTA WILD** (119886—$2.50)*

☐ **THE TRAILSMAN #7: WOLF COUNTRY** (099052—$2.25)*

☐ **THE TRAILSMAN #8: SIX-GUN DRIVE** (121724—$2.50)*

☐ **THE TRAILSMAN #9: DEAD MAN'S SADDLE** (112806—$2.25)*

☐ **THE TRAILSMAN #10: SLAVE HUNTER** (114655—$2.25)

☐ **THE TRAILSMAN #11: MONTANA MAIDEN** (116321—$2.25)

☐ **THE TRAILSMAN #12: CONDOR PASS** (118375—$2.50)*

*Prices slightly higher in Canada

Buy them at your local
bookstore or use coupon
on next page for ordering.

SIGNET Americana Novels of Interest